NATALINA REIS

INFINITE BLUE

HOT TREE PUBLISHING

For information, contact the publisher, Hot Tree Publishing.
www.hottreepublishing.com
Edited by Hot Tree Editing
Cover design by Soxsational Cover Art
Book design by Inkstain Design Studio
ISBN: 978-1-925655-89-6

10 9 8 7 6 5 4 3 2 1

MORE FROM NATALINA REIS

ROMANTIC FANTASY/PARANORMAL/SCI-FI

Desert Jewel (The Jewel Chronicles #1)

Snow Jewel (The Jewel Chronicles #2)

Lavender Fields

Heart's Prey

Infinite Blue

ROMANTIC COMEDY

We Will Always Have the Closet

Loved You Always

Blind Magic

Her Real Man

INFINITE BLUE

CHAPTER ONE

THE PULL

The Halcóns had a saying, "Once you meet him, you'll know." Shahin had never really believed it, choosing to do everything in his power to prove the absurdity of such belief. Even as he watched the other man maneuvering the blue car smoothly out of the tight space and driving away, his mind rebelled against such a notion.

Cai followed the same routine every day. He woke up at dawn and sat at the bay window, coffee in one hand, tablet in the other. By eight, his well-dressed, tall figure left the house, a woolen scarf wrapped casually around his neck, and walked down the street a couple blocks to the local Starbucks for his second cup of the morning. His car, a sensible, no-frills Corolla was always parked on the assigned parallel parking line along the sidewalk, a few doors down from his house.

From above, Shahin followed Cai's long trench coat as he entered the car, an impressive figure even from that high. The metallic blue of his car was easy to track and Shahin flew after it, a little guilt gnawing on his conscience, but curiosity and fascination for the orderly life of the man who had caught his eye had won. Who was he kidding? Cai had caught more than just his eye. The six-foot-five man with the silver hair had grabbed his heart and held it with an iron fist. Even if he wasn't aware of it at all.

Deep inside he knew. Despite a lifetime of fighting against it, believing it to be a simple old wives' tale, he knew. Cai was his soul mate.

The irony was not lost on him as he hovered over the car at a distance, the strength of the pull urging him on. The fact that they hadn't even met yet was a bit of a problem too. Stalking the man from the skies did not qualify as courtship even among Shahin's people. But was it really stalking if he didn't invade Cai's privacy, never watching him within walls? God, he hoped not, because that would brand him as a seriously creepy individual.

Cai didn't have far to go to his destination, a small building in old town Manassas. He always parked in the street and walked the few extra yards to the door of his office, a graphic artists' studio above a restaurant. Before crossing the threshold, the tall man took a last long sip of his coffee, threw the cup in the trash can by the door, and pointing his keys toward the car, locked it.

Shahin circled over the building, the need to follow Cai inside burning in his chest. Not even the cold wind, buffeting his face and body, distracted him from the larger-than-life attraction—the magnetic pull of a soul mate. He circled around a few more times, a strange, longing sound escaping his throat, before spiraling upwards and away. It was time he met his mate.

CHAPTER TWO

BLIND DATES & CHANCE MEETINGS

Cranky didn't even start to describe how Cai woke up that morning. The day ahead loomed over his horizon like a large bird of prey ready to pounce on him. Why hadn't he said no? Why was it always so hard for him to say no to his sister? All she had to do was bat her thick lashes and he was lost.

A little witch is what she is. But he loved her and was hopeless against those baby blue eyes of hers.

He was going to suck it up and be a man. How bad could it be? He would go to the assigned meeting place, meet this guy his sister was so excited about, and if he was as bad as Cai thought he was, all he had to do was make some excuse and flee the scene. Memories of the last time his sister tried to set him up with someone flooded his mind. He remembered a red-purplish face as his date emphatically declared himself "very straight" many times over. Lyra had assumed the man to be gay and had been determined to pair them together.

Oh shit. This could be bad.

By the time he left his house, his bad mood had reached fever pitch, and if anyone was unfortunate enough to approach him, he was afraid he would eat them alive. There were very few things he hated more than blind dates. He was not exactly someone who qualified as a hot number. Even though he was in his midthirties, his hair had gone silver many years back, and he wore it as a protective shield against possible disastrous relationships.

On his way to the restaurant where he was to meet the amazing Shahin—his sister's words—he decided he needed some strong coffee if he was to survive the humiliation of another failed attempt at romance. It hadn't been a bed of roses for him since Jack, his boyfriend of many years, had made the startling announcement he'd met the love of his life. As if the shock of betrayal had not been enough, Jack announced—shortly after the breakup when Cai's heart was still hemorrhaging—that he was marrying his high school sweetheart, a woman Jack had frequently referred to as *only a friend.*

Starbucks was on the way, a beacon of promised comfort and relief. A cup of good coffee had always been his self-medication— nothing a good cup of java wouldn't cure. The line was long and the room was packed with the usual crowd, a mixture of college students, writers, and a few moms with their toddlers in tow. As Cai waited for his turn, he scanned the room. He loved people-reading, a term his sister had coined a few years ago after realizing that was one of her brother's favorite pastimes.

"You should talk to people, interact," she had said, her protective sisterly claws fully out. "Instead, you sit there watching them."

"Anthropologists have been doing it for a long time." His usual comeback.

"Anthropologists actually interact with the people they're studying, bro. What you do is just a bit creepy. And definitely sad."

She wasn't wrong. It was a little pathetic that a thirty-five-year-old would be satisfied to sit in a coffee shop observing people and life happening around him without ever stepping in to participate. Satisfied was not the right word for it though. Cai feared what may happen if he stepped out of his comfort zone. He had taken a chance with Jack and look what it got him—nothing but heartache.

A deep blue caught his eye from across the coffee shop. A pair of amazing eyes met his scrutiny with a take-a-good-look-I-dare-you glint. Cai's first instinct was to look away, but he couldn't, captured and paralyzed by the electrifying vibe the man with the deep ocean eyes was emitting. The man—younger than him—had short honey-colored hair that spiked slightly on top and left his face and neck exposed. An intricate black ink tattoo stretched down the side of his neck to hide underneath the plain white T-shirt he was wearing, only to emerge again from below the short sleeves and down his well-defined biceps.

Were those roses? Cai's body caught on fire as the desire to trace the edges of the tattooed flowers grew to alarming heights. He stuck his hands in his jeans pockets, trying to control the itch on his restless fingers. The strange man with the bottomless eyes was still staring at him, caressing without touching, tender and passionate all at the same time.

"Can I take your order?"

The voice startled him and Cai looked away momentarily, placing his order for a flat white. When he looked back, those eyes were still glued to him. Cai swallowed hard as his admirer licked his lips.

I need a cold shower right now.

The phone vibrated in his pocket. Reluctantly, he pulled it out and answered. "Yes?"

The other man was still staring at him with a fire that defied the laws of physics, for it soothed as much as it burned.

"Are you there yet?" It was his sister. There where? Then he remembered.

"On my way," he lied. "Stopped for liquid courage."

"For God's sake, Cai. You sound like you're walking to the gallows." Sometimes he wished Lyra didn't read so much. She didn't talk like normal people her age.

"I might as well be, Lyra." He stole a quick glance across the room to check if the handsome stranger was still there. He was.

God, Cai was the arrow in a compass and he was the North Pole. Irreversibly and powerfully attracted.

"Don't embarrass me by not showing up, Cai." He had almost forgotten about his sister on the other end of the phone line. "He's my coworker's cousin. Please, bro. I promise I won't ever try to set you up again."

Not that he believed her, but it was a very tempting proposal. "Okay, I promise. I'm leaving right now."

Hanging up, he took a couple slow breaths, trying to get in control of his body. Good thing he was wearing a long duster coat he could use to disguise how much the stranger affected him. Cai held the coat by the edges, wrapped it closely around him, and grabbed the coffee cup to leave. As he walked by the object of his sudden madness, the other man's sexy full lips stretched into a wicked smile, releasing a million butterflies in Cai's chest.

How would it feel to touch my lips to his? The coldness of the silver snake bite he wore on his lower lip rubbing against Cai's unadorned mouth and tongue would be as thrilling as exploring the muscles barely hidden under the T-shirt. Cai shook his head and made himself lower his eyes to the floor. Like it or not, he had committed to this blasted blind date, and he was not one to renege on his promises.

Just as he was about to walk past, the stranger reached out quickly and handed him a business card. "Call me."

Cai stopped breathing and watched, mesmerized, as the other

guy licked his lips, tongue lingering over the silver ornament, inviting and tantalizing. Card firmly held between his fingers, Cai walked out of the coffee shop, still holding his breath for fear of screaming in frustration, and rushed down the street toward the restaurant where he was to meet this coworker's cousin, Shahin.

Better get this over and done. Then I can call that sex god and.... And what exactly? He hadn't dated much and was out of practice in these matters. He slid the card into his coat pocket. He would look at it later after this special kind of torture was over.

The waiter took him to the reserved table as soon as he arrived. "Mr. Halcón hasn't arrived yet," he announced in an overly formal tone. "Can I bring you something to drink?"

Cai ordered a beer and prepared himself mentally for the usual boredom of unwanted dates with their awkward small talk and constant desire to run. His mind was already fleeing to the Starbucks up the street and a certain blue-eyed man.

"Cai Banes?" The deep throaty voice woke him from his reverie.

He looked up, not believing his eyes. Standing in front of him was the man Cai had been daydreaming about, the one who seemed to have the power to elicit feelings he had almost forgotten and make him want more. So much more.

"You're Shahin?" Cai stood up on wobbly legs, forcing the words out from a desert-dry mouth.

Shahin's wicked smile made a reappearance and Cai's insides

melted as desire ran through his veins, hot and thick as lava.

"So very pleased to meet you." Shahin reached out to shake Cai's hand but instead held it still in a cocoon of warmth and promise. "Looking forward to getting to know you better."

Cai allowed himself a moment of pure delight, and smiled. Yes, he was looking forward to it as well. In the meantime, he was going to nominate Lyra for sister of the year and never, ever doubt her judgment again.

The tall man sat across from Cai, opening a napkin and draping it over his lap with a devastatingly sexy smile. "I have a confession to make." His lips parted, revealing a row of perfect white teeth in severe contrast with the subtle pink. "I knew who you were when we were at Starbucks."

The server handed Cai a menu, preventing him from reacting to Shahin's revelation. Briefly distracted, Cai thanked the server and perused the menu for a few seconds. Then he lifted his eyes to the man across from him and was surprised to meet his intense gaze. "How? We've never met, have we?" He would remember, surely.

Shahin laughed softly. "No, we haven't. I saw a picture of you." Cai was still confused. Where had he seen it? "My cousin had a picture from some office function you attended with your sister."

Comprehension dawned. "From last year's Christmas party. Yes, I came with her after being threatened with certain death should I fail to follow orders." Cai laughed. "My sister can be very persuasive."

"Was the funky sweater her idea also?" Shahin threw him a look from beneath half-closed lids and he felt the flames of desire beginning to scorch him again.

Red-hot blood rushed to Cai's face. He hoped the other man would think he was embarrassed about the god-awful Christmas sweater his sister had persuaded him to wear that night. "Yeah, that would have been her bright idea too. Ugly sweater contest. She was determined to win."

"Did you win?" Shahin waved the server over to take our orders.

"No, believe it or not, there were even worse knitted aberrations at that party." He put the menu down beside his plate and looked at the young server. "This beer will do, thanks."

Shahin's eyebrows arched in surprise. "No wine? They have a Portuguese white that's to die for." Cai shook his head. He was not much of a wine drinker. In fact, he was not much of a drinker at all. The occasional beer was as far as he went when it came to alcohol. Shahin shrugged and looked up at the waiter. "Bring a bottle of Muralhas, please."

After ordering, Cai watched as the waiter rushed to the kitchen a little flushed. Had he felt Shahin's raw appeal as well? He could almost see waves of pheromones wafting from the younger man's body and radiating around him like heat. Cai slipped a finger between the collar and his neck, suddenly needing more air.

"I understand you've lived here most of your life." How much information had Lyra given this man about him? It didn't seem fair that he had so little information about Shahin—even if it was his own fault for not wanting to know. "It's strange because both you and your sister have unusual names."

Cai chuckled. "Not that strange when your parents are huge fantasy geeks. Good thing they stopped at two children, or we may have ended up with a brother named Gandalf." Shahin laughed with him. "And you?"

"My family and I move around a bit, but we always seem to end up here in Northern Virginia," Shahin said, fiddling with his snake bite. Cai followed the man's fingers with his eyes and involuntarily licked his lips, heat spreading through his body again. "We're strange birds who tend to flock together." Amused by his own words, Shahin laughed softly before continuing, "I was born up north in Canada, but I come south almost every year for the winter."

"For work?"

"You could say that." The waiter came back with the bottle of wine. Cai covered a smile as the young man's hand shook and he spilled some of the wine onto the tablecloth. Cai was not the only one affected by the wild creature across from him. Shahin seemed oblivious to it. "I must visit my local customers yearly."

The server took the bottle away, white complexion tinted red. "What do you do for a living?" Cai was very curious now.

"I'm in charge of the company that supports my family business.

Cyber-marketing mostly."

Shahin didn't look like a businessman; too casual and young-looking to be a CEO of anything other than maybe a rock band. For the second time, Cai stared fascinated at the other man's tattoo, a black-ink profusion of roses starting by his right ear and spreading down the slope of his neck and under his T-shirt. Both ears sported plain flat black studs that covered his earlobes, and his outfit, a simple pairing of a white T-shirt and light blue jeans, did not evoke the image of an executive of any kind.

Lost in his visual assessment, Cai was startled when a hot briny smell assailed his senses. The discomfited waiter had placed a large bowl of steamy mussels in front of both of them and went back to the kitchen as fast as his legs could carry him. It looked delicious but paled in comparison with his table companion's lips and blue infinity eyes. Those amazing eyes held his captive and made him wish things he had not wished or wanted in years.

"You have the most amazing eyes I've ever seen," Shahin said suddenly, snapping Cai out of the semitrance holding him hostage. "Are they green?"

Cai had never thought of his eyes as anything other than ordinary. "Hazel—at least, that's what my driver's license says." Was the god with the Greek-sea eyes really praising *his* eyes? He swallowed a nervous knot in his throat and slurped a mussel into his mouth, hoping the shell would disguise his agitation.

"Do you know that green eyes are the rarest color?" Shahin's eyes were fixed on Cai's. "Only two percent of people in the world have green eyes. In other words, you're unique."

Cai coughed, the juice from the mussel spilling across his lips and chin. Feeling like he had lost all sense of control, he wiped his mouth with the napkin. What was it about this man that made a calm, always-in-control man like him lose his composure with a single glance? Shahin was handsome, yes, but he met and talked to handsome men every day in his job and he had never once turned into a bumbling idiot.

"And your hair—" Shahin threw his hands up in the air as if in surrender. "It's absolutely one of a kind. How long have you had white hair?"

Normally any call of attention to his prematurely white hair would have him bristling, but coming from Shahin, it sounded flattering. He chuckled instead. "It started turning when I was in high school. It's a family trait apparently. Looking ancient at thirty-five is not exactly hip."

"Never dated a silver fox." Dated? Was he considering dating Cai? Shahin studied him for a moment, eyes sliding from his white hair to his eyes and then focusing on his lips for a moment longer than necessary. Cai swallowed hard again. "I like it."

As the meal progressed, Cai soon regretted having ordered such messy food. Being around Shahin seemed to bring out the clumsy in him, as the multiple stains on his shirt and the constant dripping of juices down his chin attested. By the time they left the restaurant, he was sure he smelled like a giant walking mussel. His attentive companion followed him outside and walked with him up the street toward the same Starbucks where they had met earlier.

"I'd like to see you again," Shahin said, stopping by a black motorcycle parked in front of the coffee shop. He took a step closer until he was standing within arm's reach of Cai, setting blood into a wild race through his heart. "I have an event tomorrow and the next day. Can we meet Monday? I can pick you up here." He laughed, his eyes roaming Cai's body. "I will think of this Starbucks as our place from now on."

Cai liked that. He had always been levelheaded with his feet firmly rooted to the ground. Solid, Jack always called him. In other words, boring. Otherwise, why would Jack have left him after all the years together? It was exciting and heartwarming to have someone interested in him again.

Shahin slid his hand along Cai's arm sending shivers up and down his spine. Then he climbed on the motorcycle, put on a helmet, and started the engine. The motor idled into a purr and Shahin smiled before pulling the visor down to cover his face. With a wave he was off, riding down the street and vanishing around the corner.

Cai wondered why he could still hear the purring of the motor, and was startled to discover it was his heart strumming away inside his chest. The same heart that he thought had bled to death had somehow come back to life.

"MOST WOMEN MY AGE ARE grandmothers by now." The moaned complaint was not unexpected. Every year when the family moved south for a few months, Shahin's mother suffered from what he called "broody spells"—the overwhelming, however annoying, urge to hatch another baby. Since she could no longer have children, her broody eyes turned to her middle son and the only one who had so far failed to reproduce.

"Mom, how many times have I told you I'm not spawning anytime soon?" He was not heartless, and there was a part of him that felt bad for her. He would never have children—not his own anyway. But she already had five grandchildren. Both his younger sister and older brother had mated some years ago. Maya had two boys and Sal two girls and a baby boy. Why did she need any more?

"You're breaking my heart, fledgling." His mother, who didn't look a year older than forty, made a big production of hunching over like an old hag while grasping at her chest. "I will die without ever holding one of your babies."

Shahin rolled his eyes. "Really, Mom? You look younger than me. You're not dying anytime soon." He threw his hands up in the air and turned around to leave. "Give me a break. You know I'm gay, so why torture yourself—and me—by wishing for something that's never going to happen?"

Not waiting to hear her answer, Shahin left, slamming the door behind him. It made him mad when his mother tried to guilt him into mating with a female. He had never hidden his homosexuality from her—or anybody. Ever. As soon as he fully realized he was attracted to other men rather than women, he had laid it all out for his family and friends. Shahin didn't want to lead the girls that flocked around him on by giving them even the slightest hope he would one day pick one of them to mate and breed with. But his mother always went back to it. He was letting the family down. How hard would it be to make a baby? He could always go back to his ways afterward. He growled at the memory of the dozens of conversations he'd had with his mother.

It was almost five o'clock and he could already feel the pull. Uncanny how his body knew where his soul mate was and urged him to go to him. Yes, he had always been told about the pull of the soul mate, the one who completed you, filled the void in your heart. Shahin had dismissed it as a fairy tale, but he knew better now. The pull was so strong he found it hard to control the need to run, to fly to Cai.

He could only imagine the reaction he'd get from the other man if he showed up at his workplace and declared his love for him.

They had just met, and even though Cai was most definitely not impervious to his charm and boyish good looks, no one in their right mind would take Shahin seriously. Hell, *he* was having trouble taking himself seriously. Shahin wondered what excuse he could possibly come up with to "accidentally" stumble across the other man.

His family had nested some ways from old downtown, in a new development that boasted wooded lots and privacy. The Halcóns treasured their privacy, so they had picked their homes both in Virginia and Canada in giant lots from where the neighbors could only be guessed at, not seen. At first, the whole family had roosted together under the same roof. It was a massive place, big enough to house the many members of Shahin's family comfortably. But Shahin craved his own privacy. He had always been the "wild" one, the one who was in trouble and fought the rules with all his might. So he had moved into his own place. A tiny older house on a farm, a healthy distance from his family's. Now he wished he had rented an old flat in town instead, so he would have the perfect excuse to cross paths with Cai anytime he wished.

He climbed on his motorcycle—the black devil, he called it— and headed into town. The traffic was quickly getting heavier as rush hour approached. Shahin wanted to make sure he wouldn't miss his soul mate. Cai lived just a few minutes' drive from downtown, in a newer townhouse in the outskirts of Manassas. Shahin wanted to get to him before he headed home.

At that time of the day, it wasn't hard to find a parking place by the train station, just a few yards away from the other man's work. Shahin checked himself for dead bugs and removed a reddish feather from his shoulder. *Damn! I'm shedding again.* An unwelcome side effect of taking so long to find a mate, his mother always told him. *Bullshit.* His mother would say just about anything to make him reconsider his non-choices. It would be funny if it wasn't so annoying.

As he crossed to the opposite side of the rail tracks, he saw him. Cai had just stepped out of the building and was immersed in conversation with a man Shahin didn't recognize. His sharp eyes zoomed in on the duo and examined the man with a small measure of trepidation. What was he scared of anyway? He knew Cai was into him. The way he felt when they touched hands, the way the other man's eyes smoldered when they met his. Still—

"Hey, Cai," he called from a few feet away, waving in greeting. "What a surprise. What are you doing here?" Man, he should have gone into theater or law, as good as he was at lying and pretending.

Cai lifted his amazing hazel eyes in recognition and smiled. The need to run and kiss those luscious lips took Shahin by storm, and he bit down on his tongue to control himself. He tasted blood. "Shahin! What—? I work here. You?"

Shahin laughed under his breath at the other man's flustered response. So he *did* have an effect on him. Good.

"I came downtown for some ice cream. I hear that Jitterbugs

is the place to go for out-of-this-world iced treats." *I'm so full of shit, I'm surprised the flies aren't swarming around me.* Shahin stopped a couple steps away and threw a sideways glance at the second man, a rather handsome guy who stared at Shahin suspiciously. Shahin extended his hand to him. "Hi. I'm Shahin Halcón."

Cai shook his head. "I'm so sorry. Shahin, this is Ted Willard." Shahin arched his eyebrows. "He's a coworker and friend of the family."

He had hoped for a "he's a customer" or a business acquaintance. Friend of the family hinted at deeper connections, something Shahin was irrationally jealous of.

"Nice meeting you, Ted." He turned his attention to Cai, a smile on his lips and a craving in his heart. "Would you like to join me for ice cream? Or coffee?" There was a great coffee house just around the corner.

Shahin ignored the murderous looks he was getting from the man next to Cai as his soul mate had a moment of total confusion and hesitation. "I— Not sure—" He looked at his friend and smiled apologetically. "Sorry, Ted. We'll go for drinks another day if you don't mind. There is something important I must discuss with Shahin."

Shahin was not the only bullshitter after all. He tucked in his chin, trying to hide the amused smile that crept onto his lips. He gestured a noncommittal wave at the departing man and then sighed deeply as Ted walked away, the heaviness of his steps betraying his dissatisfaction with the sudden turn of events.

"We have something important to talk about?" He couldn't help but teasing Cai, who wrapped the scarf tighter around his neck, disguising the light blush that spread across his face. "Shall we discuss it over ice cream or coffee?"

Cai laughed. "Considering it's like forty degrees out here, coffee might be a better choice."

They fell into step side by side, Shahin's hand itching to breach the space between them and touch Cai. "Boyfriend of yours?" Shahin bit his tongue. *Why am I asking him this? Stupid.*

The other man raised his eyebrows and glanced at Shahin, his step faltering for a nanosecond. "Who? Ted?" Shahin shrugged. "No—well, once. We dated a long time ago. We were kids." He chuckled softly and stared ahead. "He was my first—"

Not good. Not good at all. First boyfriends were always unforgettable. Either they had been so bad you couldn't erase them out of your memories, or they were the end of innocence and would forever sport a halo of magic. That they were still on friendly terms meant Ted was one of the latter. Shahin had quite a long list of past relationships, but he would never forget his first. *I'll have to woo him with extra charm.*

The problem was, he was not the charming kind. Handsome, even hot if you believed some of his past dates, and interesting. But charming?

The coffee shop was just around the corner. Inside, the fire was roaring and music played softly in the background. They ordered a couple coffees and sat down side by side on the sofa by the fireplace.

Halloween decorations cluttered the walls and tables, tiny ghosts and witch's hats sprinkled around the coffeehouse. Cai had removed his overcoat and folded it neatly over the arm of the couch, careful not to disturb a two-foot tall witch standing next to it. Shahin watched him, an amused smile dancing on his lips. Cai's eyes caught on his and he raised an eyebrow.

"Are you laughing at me?" his soul mate asked, his luscious lips curling upward.

"You're just so—tidy." Shahin immediately regretted the words. They sounded judgmental, as if he thought Cai was an old, fussy man instead of the beautiful creature he really was. "I didn't mean it the way it sounded. I'm pretty messy. You look organized and methodical."

Cai laughed, throwing his head backward. "You have a gift to make a compliment sound like an insult. I am organized. I have to be. When you grow up with responsibilities and people who depend on you, you have no choice but to step up to the plate."

"Are you insinuating I don't have any responsibilities?" Shahin made a production at pretending he was offended. The other man only laughed harder. "What? Really? You have such a low opinion of me?" He laughed along.

"Sorry, Shahin. But the snake bite and all the tattoos don't scream responsibility." Cai managed to control his laughter, but the smile lingered in his lips. "I'm being terribly judgmental and I apologize. Am I wrong though? I'm curious."

Shahin took a long sip of his coffee while sneaking a glance at the man beside him. Laughter had caused him to tear up just enough to make his eyes glint like emeralds in the sun. Shahin swallowed the knot that had formed in his throat, his body coming suddenly alive with the yearning he always felt in Cai's presence.

"No, I supposed you're not." Why lie? Shahin had never been the obedient, super reliable or duty-bound man in his flock. He was the one who argued with all the elders, refused to go along with the traditions and rules of his people, and never felt the slightest tinge of guilt for not doing what his mom and family felt he should do. "The tattoos were to spite my oldest brother and the snake bite to piss off my mom."

Cai cleared his throat. "Are you saying you only do things to make somebody else mad at you? Do you even like your tattoos?"

He had to give it a minute's thought before answering. "Hell, I do love my tattoos, but you're right. I got them done just to piss off Sal." Shahin laughed. "Jesus, I'm an idiot. I've spent most of my life striving to make others raving mad at me and never realized it until just now."

The other man looked confused, his gorgeous eyes blinking at the speed of light. *He probably thinks I'm nuts.* And he wouldn't be totally wrong.

Shahin sobered and took another gulp of coffee. "Sorry, Cai. You must be wishing you never accepted my invite for coffee."

"Nobody can say you're boring, that's for sure," Cai said, a crooked smile on his lips. "You must lead an interesting life."

Boring until I met you. "Not really." Throwing caution to the wind, Shahin reached out for Cai's hand. He started, but didn't pull his hand away. Cai's skin was soft and warm under the cocoon of his, but his hand was large and strong. Shivers of pleasure ran up and down his spine as he tightened the hold around the other man's fingers and stroked him with his thumb. He leaned closer and lowered his voice. "I want to see you again."

Cai's breathing was audibly rapid and he trembled under Shahin's touch. "We're very different."

"Does it matter? We have a connection." Shahin slid his fingers under Cai's hand and caressed the sensitive skin of his palm. The other man pulled his hand away as if he'd been electrocuted. Feeling empty and oddly bereft, Shahin hid his hands in his pockets. "I know you've felt it too. There is something strong pulling us together." *Shit! Too early.* He was going to scare Cai away.

Cai was silent for a moment, his eyes lowered, breathing fast. "Shahin, we barely know each other—"

"Aren't you attracted to me?" *Hell, why am I so fucking impulsive?* "Look at me and tell me you aren't."

His soul mate looked up then, his bright eyes burning a hole into his, melting his heart and making his blood race through his body at the speed of lightning. "I'm attracted to a lot of guys. It doesn't mean I want or will date them all." *Ouch! Knife straight to where it hurts the most, my ego.*

Forcing himself to go slow, Shahin took a deep breath before replying. "Sorry. That came out totally wrong. I'm impulsive, to put it mildly, and often say the exact opposite of what I should. But I would like to see you again." Yearning to touch Cai's hand again, Shahin sat on his. "No pressure, no rush. Just two people getting to know each other."

Cai seemed to hesitate for a moment, as if trying to decide whether the rather unconventional man across from him was worth the effort and investment. Then his face opened and Shahin's stomach finally settled, the buzzing of a million wasps silenced by the light and generosity of the other man's smile. He could breathe again.

"You realize I'm older than you." Cai flattened his hand over his heart, a self-deprecating expression on his face. That man had no idea how handsome and sexy he was. No idea how his mere presence could trigger fireworks inside Shahin's body and melt his guts like lava.

Shahin chuckled, rubbing his hands against the side of his pants in an attempt at diffusing the electric shimmer that made them shake almost uncontrollably. "Yes, you're ancient. I bet you remember the civil war."

The awkwardness of a few moments before gone, the two men sat companionably side by side on the sofa, cradling their coffees in their hands and chatting about everything and anything. For the first time in a long while, Shahin's restless soul was at peace, happy and contented in the presence of the one who completed him.

CHAPTER THREE

FLYING & FALLING

Lyra had that expression that he always equated to the Cheshire cat's. Cai sneaked a look at her from the corner of his eye, not wanting to invite what he could guess would be a tirade about his dating life. The subterfuge didn't work. Her feline grin expanded to alarming widths. He could almost hear the words gurgling up her throat, ready to explode out of her mouth.

"I'm not dating him." He wasn't. Shahin was an interest, a friend—one he would admittedly love to rip the clothes off and get to know up close and personal, but they were not dating. Not yet. Maybe never. "I'm not. Don't look at me like that, sis."

His sister covered the space between them with a graceful leap and wrapped her arms around his neck. "I'm so happy for you, Cai. It's about time you have someone in your life again."

Despite his annoyance, Cai laughed at his sister's excitement. You would think he had just won the Nobel Prize. "Will you stop being so weird about this? We had coffee, that's all."

"Coffee is a gateway drug for romance." Still hanging from his neck, Lyra opened her saucer-like eyes like two beacons of light. "Is he cute?" A tiny smile crept to his lips and she squealed. "He's hot, right? Smoking hot?"

Cai unwrapped her arms from around his neck and pushed her away gently. "He's handsome, yes." His voice went down to a whisper. "And young."

"You dog! You're dating a younger guy? How young is he? Twenty?"

"Jesus, Lyra. He's probably in his midtwenties. I'm just guessing. Just younger than me." Now free from his sister's arms, Cai sat by the high kitchen counter and picked a donut from the brown box his sister had brought with her. They were still warm and gooey perfection.

Lyra came around to the other side of the counter and snatched the donut from his hand. "You know that's my favorite flavor, bro." Before he could protest, she took a giant bite out of it and laughed at him, her chipmunk cheeks swollen with the pastry. "It's not like you're old, Cai. You're only thirty-five. Hardly a silver fox."

After a perfunctory look-over, Cai decided for the plain yeast donut. "He looks like a kid, snake bite and all."

Lyra choked on the donut, coughing out bits and pieces into her napkin. "Wait! What? He wears a snake bite?" He could almost hear her thoughts. *That is so unlike the type you normally go for, bro.* She meant the boring, fastidious older men he always seemed to attract. "Wow, I don't know whether to be impressed or worried. That's a serious shift in preferences, Cai. Are you going through a midlife crisis already?"

Cai stopped midway through bringing the donut to his mouth and stared at her, eyebrows raised high. "What are you talking about?"

"You know, some guys buy a sports car, others date hip younger guys...." She said it with a devilish smile on her lips, knowing all too well it would not only rattle him just so, but also make him second-guess himself. "Come on! You know I'm joking, right? I'm just surprised. Until now your boyfriends have been the sensible kind. Shahin does not sound at all like that."

He chewed on the donut pensively. "I guess not," he said after swallowing the pastry. "He seems impulsive and a bit on the wild side." He fell silent again, his eyes focused on nothing in particular. "But there is something between us." It was a whisper, a thought.

Lyra was not smiling anymore, her eyes trained on her brother's always serious face. "What kind of thing?"

He raised his eyes to hers, almost surprised she was still there. "I don't know. I can't explain it. A pull—strong and insistent. Never felt anything like it. It's bit intimidating."

His sister placed a hand on his shoulder and squeezed lightly. "For once don't think so much and just follow your heart."

His past relationships hadn't been a great success. Ted had been his first boyfriend when they were both seniors in high school. Even then his jet-black hair was already turning silver, something that made him an outcast of sorts. Or maybe it was his introverted personality that kept him apart from the other young people. Ted had been the president of the art club and had taken a shine to the young, quiet, artistic man he was back then. They dated for a few months until they parted ways to go to college. Their friendship had remained intact through the years and when the chance presented itself to work together, it had seemed the natural thing to do. Every relationship Cai had had since then had ended in a non-dramatic way, the two of them choosing to go their own way. Until Jack.

"And don't even think about your idiot ex." Sometimes Cai thought his sister could read his mind. "He was a sexually confused moron who couldn't tell a good thing if it bit him in the ass. You deserve so much better than he could ever be." Then why did he feel like a loser?

Donuts all gone, Lyra perched on the counter, her long skinny legs half dangling from the high stool and covered in goose bumps. "Aren't you cold?" Silly question. She was obviously cold, her legs left bare by the shortest of denim shorts she was wearing. "Why are you wearing shorts in this weather?"

She picked up a chunk of leftover donut and threw it at him. "Because pants are too restrictive. Besides, remember what Mom used to say." At his quizzical look, she offered, "If you know you got it, strut it." Amused at her own words, Lyra threw her head backward and laughed.

She could be just as annoying as funny and sweet. His little sister, maybe not so little anymore. She was just slightly shorter than he was, thin and shapely in all the places that drove men crazy over her. Not that she cared. She had eyes only for her longtime boyfriend, Zack. They had been dating since college, seven years and counting.

"Doesn't Zack mind that you *strut your stuff*?" The man was possibly the most patient boyfriend Cai had ever met, putting up with his sister's antics like a champ.

Lyra waved a hand in the air dismissively. "I didn't have anything clean to wear, thus the shorts. I've been busy with the foundation and didn't notice that my last pair of clean pants had just hit the hamper."

Cai laughed. "You're a slob. How does Zack put up with you?"

"Apparently a golden tongue and bedroom skills can move mountains." He cringed. Why did she insist on talking about her sex life with him? There ought to be a law against sisters doing that. "Don't give me that face. The golden tongue is good for more than just talking—" She winked at him suggestively and he gagged. Her laughter spilled out of her lips and into the air around them. She was awful. "You're such a prude, Cai."

"I'm not a prude. I do, however, have much better common sense than you." Cai collected the empty box and dropped it in the trash can across from the counter. "Are you coming with me today?"

Lyra's raven black hair, tied in a bun on top of her head, shook along with her. "No, not today. Not only am I not dressed for the occasion, but I need to do some laundry before Zack gets home." She collected her bag from the couch and turned around to wink at her brother. "Mind you, not that I'm planning on wearing much when he gets home from his work trip tonight." Not waiting to hear Cai's protest, she left, closing the door behind her.

Cai shook his head. She'd never learn. He was expected at St. Francis's very soon, but he couldn't leave until all the dishes were clean and put away. Lyra often told him he was an old lady trapped in the body of a young man. Even though he knew she was only teasing, there was some truth to her assessment. He had always been what his loving mom had called an old soul—mature ahead of his years, somewhat of a loner, always feeling a bit out of place. Order appealed to him as chaos appealed to others, and the idea of a quiet day with a book was so much more attractive to him than a day out at a concert or an evening in a bar.

When he finally left the house, putting on his overcoat as he walked down the street to the church, Cai felt the hairs on the back of his neck stand up. He turned around to check whether he was being watched or followed, but the street was practically empty. He shook his head, trying to dispel the strange feeling from his mind and body, and kept walking. As he approached the side door of St.

Francis's, where he often came to help with charity work, he thought he heard a loud screech coming from above. He looked up in time to see a shadow of a large bird—could it be a hawk?—fly high above and just beyond his line of sight. Strange place for a bird of prey to be hovering, but it wasn't the first time he had spotted a hawk in the past couple weeks. Nature had been acting strangely for the past few years, so it shouldn't come as a surprise that even birds were beginning to behave atypically. It was still wondrous to see such a majestic creature, gracefully soaring on its amazingly powerful wings.

Night had fallen by the time the work in church was finished. They had successfully allocated clothes, furniture, and other useful wares to several neighborhood families in need. Cai had been helping with this project since he was a kid. His mother and father—when his workload allowed—had brought him and Lyra along every month for the church's charity drive. Cai affectionately recalled car trips with his mother and a whiny sister, driving around town trying to solicit donations from local wealthy families and businesses. He didn't do that part of the job anymore because of lack of time, but he rarely missed the monthly meeting at the church for packing and distribution of wares. Lyra called him St. Cai as a joke, but she herself was the head of a local foundation that did a lot of charity work. The apple didn't fall too far from the tree, it seemed.

He pulled the collar up to protect his neck from the chill of the night and crossed his arms, preparing for the short walk to his house.

A sudden breeze on his back made him shiver and look behind him. Nothing. He was becoming paranoid in his old age, it seemed.

His mind wandered to Shahin's handsome face, eyes as deep as the ocean and just as mysterious, and he immediately felt the stirrings of desire. The irreverent man wouldn't leave his thoughts, haunting his dreams and following him around all through the day. Cai had caught himself daydreaming about Shahin even in the middle of work that normally would hold his full attention.

Another blast of cold air made him turn around again. A swoosh of great wings blew his short hair out of place. A hawk! Did hawks fly at night? In the middle of a residential area? Was that hawk following him? He shook the ridiculous idea out of his head and stared at the great hawk soaring into the dark skies above. He hugged himself as a shiver ran through his body. *Exhaustion is playing tricks with my mind.* Cai resumed his walk toward the house, a strange and inexplicable sense of both unease and pleasure taking over his senses. That blast of air had felt like a caress. He laughed at his own whimsical thoughts. *Next, you're going to believe the zombie apocalypse is imminent. I got to get some sleep.*

He sped up, anxious to get home and into bed. He hadn't slept much at all since meeting Shahin. It was as if their meeting had unsettled his whole self, his peace of mind. There was a constant sense of urgency in his heart now, Shahin's attractive face always dancing before his eyes, teasing and calling him. After years of lukewarm love affairs, he couldn't be sure whether these unexpected feelings for the unconventional man were a welcome change.

SHAHIN USUALLY TOOK A DETOUR so he could enjoy the exhilarating feeling of the wind beneath his wings, lifting him up, propelling him farther into the dark skies above. But tonight, he wanted to get home as fast as he could. Following Cai had not been the best idea he had ever had. The very proximity of the one who completed him made him jittery with desire, a pull so strong he had almost landed on the other man's shoulder so he could touch him. Now his body burned beneath his feathers. He contemplated taking a quick dip in the river but dismissed the idea quickly. It was not safe for a hawk to be out this late. Great horned owls had a taste for hawk flesh and they could see a lot better in the dark.

His body morphed into human form even before his talons touched the ground right in front of his house, sheltered from others by a wall of thick trees. Stark naked, Shahin opened his unlocked front door and, neglecting to turn on the lights, ran up the stairs to his bedroom. He wanted to close his eyes and dream of his soul mate. Without bothering to put on any clothes, Shahin slipped between the cool cotton sheets, a comforting hug of sorts. He sighed, grasped his pillow, and buried his face in it.

In the darkness, Cai's handsome face appeared, his luminous green eyes quizzical as usual. Shahin wondered whether Cai ever got the answers to all the questions he always seemed to have. He liked that in his soul mate—that thirst for knowledge, curiosity for life. However, he realized that some of that was a reflection of his lack of confidence, his lack of trust in himself. Shahin was determined to change that. For now, he focused on the way Cai's skin crinkled around his eyes as he attempted to make sense of what he saw or felt. His gut tightened as he followed the trail from Cai's eyes to his mouth, the generous full lips he so wanted to kiss. His skin, rubbing against the softness of the sheets, shivered and puckered in pleasure. A moan escaped his lips as he swelled against the linen.

Shit, not now.

He plopped onto his back, focusing his eyes on the high ceiling of his room. His supersharp eyesight could distinguish every dent, every imperfection on the surface of the ceiling even in the dark, but he couldn't see what he wanted to see the most—Cai. With another flop, Shahin rolled out of bed and almost ran to the bathroom. A cold shower seemed to be in order.

Without hesitation, Shahin jumped under the cold running water with a gasp. Once his body got used to the temperature, he leaned on the tiled wall behind the showerhead and allowed his thoughts to run back to Cai. Big mistake. As soon as the tall, silver-haired man wavered into existence in his mind, Shahin was hard again.

This is going to be a long night.

"ARE YOU SURE IT'S A good idea?" Cai had not seen Ted approach his desk. His old friend's eyebrows were knitted tightly and his lips stretched into a thin line of worry.

"What do you mean? Is the design really that bad?" Cai pointed at the sketch he was working on, an idea for a local store logo. He was confused. He had gone over his idea with Ted just the day before, and the man hadn't said anything then.

"Not the design," Ted said, waving a hand in front of him. "That's perfect. I'm talking about you seeing that tattooed guy."

Cai's eyes opened wide. "Shahin? What's wrong with him?" In his hurry to defend the man who haunted his dreams, he had forgotten to refute the assumption he was dating him. Which he wasn't. Was he?

"He's—shifty." His friend's choice of words made him laugh. "It's not funny, Cai. There is something weird about him."

"Having tattoos and a snake bite do not a bad guy make." Cai cringed at his own words. He was starting to sound like his mother. "Come on, Ted. Be real. He's just unconventional."

"He's so much younger than you." Ted was aiming for the jugular now. He knew how sensitive Cai was about the fact his white hair made him look older than he was.

"He's a grown man like us, Ted." His voice had gone down to a near growl. He didn't want to argue, but bringing up the age factor was not only insensitive coming from a close friend but also unfair. It was bad enough the thought had occurred to him more than once ever since meeting the handsome Shahin. "Besides, we're not dating or anything."

"I saw the look he gave you." Why did everyone he cared about feel the need to treat him as if he was a little kid in need of protection? Just because he had been hurt in the past did not mean he was not able to stand on his own. "He has plans."

In spite of his annoyance, Cai laughed again. "You make him sound like Dr. Sinister." He deepened his voice to mimic a movie mad scientist. "Be afraid. Be very afraid. Dr. Sinister will snatch you from your bed and turn you into a monster."

Ted frowned, obviously not seeing the humor in the situation. "I'm telling you, Cai—there is something weird about that guy. I'm your oldest friend and I don't want to see you hurt again."

Cai jumped to his feet, propelling his wheeled chair across the room and on a crash course with Eliza's desk, who looked up, startled by the commotion. He shrugged an apology in her direction and looked back at Ted, now at eye level.

"I'm all grown up, my friend, in case you haven't noticed." He had no wish to hurt Ted's feelings. He had always been a great friend, in good times and bad, but this was getting ridiculous. "I'm no longer the shy, unsure kid you met in high school, the one who'd just come to terms with the idea of being gay. Those days are gone. I know what I'm doing." Most of the time, anyway.

The other man blinked and opened his mouth to say something, but gave up at the last minute. He raised his hands in surrender, shook his head, and walked away, mumbling something under his breath.

Cai retrieved his chair and sat down at his desk. The design he had been working on lay flat in front of him. He had been enthusiastically working on it all day, but now he had lost his focus. Shahin had again invaded and taken over his every thought. *Damn, Ted! Why did you have to bring him up?* He rolled the project and slid it into one of the cardboard cylinders he used to keep designs safe, put his pencils away, and prepared to leave. It was almost time to go home and he obviously was not going to get anything else done that afternoon. He had promised Lyra a visit, so he slipped into his overcoat, wrapped a checkered scarf around his neck, and left.

It was an especially cold day, the gray clouds hiding the autumn sun and covering the world in a blurry mantle. Cai's fingers itched with the desire to add color to a colorless day. His artistic soul had trouble dealing with days like this, when everything seemed to bleed into each other, allowing for no differences, no variety of color or shape. For his job, he mostly drew in charcoal, monochromatic artistic views of common and commercial things. But at home, when no one was looking, he pulled out his brushes and pots of paint and colored the world around him. For years he had been able to snuff that part of his soul and focus on the more realistic career-oriented talent, but his other side had made a return after the heartbreak. It made him happy to brush blues and lavenders, pinks and yellows across the blank canvas. It fed his starving heart and need for... what exactly, he didn't know.

Instead of walking the short distance to his sister's downtown apartment, he turned the other way and got in his car. He needed to go home and paint. He'd been restless ever since meeting Shahin. No, that was not true. He had been restless even before meeting him. His life, the way it had been for the past few years, was not enough for him anymore. At some point, his contentment with being alone had morphed into a need for companionship, a desire for love that eclipsed all else. But ever since the younger man had appeared this need had become desperate, urgent, and overwhelmingly strong. Cai didn't understand or care to explain it. It was unsettling and yet it filled him with an unfamiliar sense of excitement.

His painting smock was covered in familiar stains, each with a little story that both comforted and thrilled him. As he slipped his arms into its sleeves, Cai took stock of all the colors splashed haphazardly across the white surface of the garment. They were witnesses to moments of joy, moments of extreme sadness, instances of his creative mind taking him where his body and soul couldn't.

Soaring moments of escape from a life that held him captive.

His brushes carefully displayed in a big mason jar were waiting for him. Lyra had always told him he was a different man when he was painting. She had urged him to take on a career more in tune with his artistic moods, but in the end, the part of him that was reasonable and sensible had won—he had chosen an artistic career, yes, but one that was also more down-to-earth and brought a better paycheck along.

The canvas stood against the easel, right behind the big bay window of an upstairs room. The view was the main reason he had bought that house. Miles of green, grass and trees, spread before his eyes, the promise of a lake in the distance. It always soothed his soul, but today even the gorgeous greenery had little effect over the restlessness in him. Cai stood in front of the canvas, brush in hand, gaze lost on the horizon. A flutter of dark wings snapped him out of his reverie. Was that the damned hawk he kept seeing everywhere he went? *Am I going crazy?* He stepped closer to the window to check it out, but whatever had flown outside was nowhere to be seen anymore.

He had just returned to the painting when his phone rang. Cursing under his breath, he dropped the brush inside the container and pulled out his cell phone. "What?"

The voice on the other side was not his sister's as he'd thought it would be. "Cai, it's Shahin." Muted by surprise, Cai didn't respond. "Are you there? Hello?"

"Yes, I'm here," he said, finally finding his voice. "What's wrong?"

Laughter reached his ears. "Nothing's wrong. Calling to invite you out." Cai's heart skipped a beat. "It's a beautiful evening. I'd love to show you one of my favorite places in the world."

Cai thought about asking him how he had found his phone number, but then realized his sister had most likely given it to him. He stared at the beginning of his latest creation and sighed. As much as he wanted to immerse himself in it, spending some time with the man he couldn't get his mind off was too attractive an opportunity.

"Where?"

"I'm close by—your sister gave my cousin your address." Cai may have to kill his sister after all. What if Shahin had turned out to be a serial killer? "I'll pick you up in five minutes."

Putting the phone away, Cai looked at himself. He was still wearing his work clothes, casual, but too formal for a spur-of-the-moment date. He ran to the bedroom and changed into a pair of jeans and a soft blue sweater. The knock on the door came just as he wrapped a white scarf around his neck. Grabbing his peacoat on the way out, Cai took a quick look around to make sure he had turned everything off, and opened the door.

The handsome, tall figure of Shahin stood there, his adorned well-shaped lips stretching into a radiant smile, his intense blue eyes in sharp contrast with the darkness of his eyebrows. *God, he's gorgeous.* There was something wild about the way he looked, the way he moved.

Cai couldn't explain it, but he couldn't help but being attracted to that side of him—a side so disparate from his own personality. His whole body shook with a mixture of delight and agony.

"You're ready." Shahin wore a plain black leather jacket over a white T-shirt and aviator sunglasses. He hadn't shaved in a couple days, it seemed, and his thick light brown hair was disheveled as if he had just run against the wind. Cai gulped and pulled the edges of his coat tighter together. "Let's go."

Thoughts of contradicting Shahin never crossed Cai's mind. Closing the door behind him, he followed the younger man into the street. He stopped suddenly when he saw Shahin's motorcycle parked by the curb.

"We're riding on that?" Cai couldn't remember a single time he had been on a motorcycle. They scared him a bit. He felt the same way about riding horses—which he had done once or twice. The rider never seemed to be completely in control. He needed to have a measure of control, or an overwhelming discomfort took over him. He had never been able to understand people who enjoyed the feeling of—what was the opposite of being in control?

Shahin laughed. "Meet my black devil. Yes, we're riding it." He handed Cai a helmet, an amused smile dancing at the corners of his lips. "Don't tell me you've never been on one."

Cai licked his lips, suddenly embarrassed by his rather unexciting life experiences. His mouth was so dry, he couldn't say anything. He nodded instead.

"Well, you're in for a treat. It's the closest you get to flying without ever leaving the ground." Shahin stepped closer and slid the helmet gently over Cai's head, tightening it under his chin. His warm fingers brushed against Cai's skin, making it tingle at the contact. He wanted to cover it with his hand and keep it there, but that was madness. They barely knew each other. Cai had never been this unwise, this—impulsive.

Shahin had put on his own helmet, climbed on the vehicle, and started the engine. "Come on, climb on." Timidly, almost fearfully, Cai swung his right leg over the seat and settled behind the driver, the vibration of the motor pushing him even closer to Shahin's body. There was no avoiding it. His body responded immediately to the contact, and there was no way the other man couldn't tell, smashed together as they were. Cai braced himself for an embarrassing remark, but surprisingly none came. Instead, the younger man revved up the engine and sent them flying down the road.

Cai held on for dear life at first, his dislike for motorcycles overwhelming him. His knuckles turned white as he grasped the other man's jacket. But as the wind rushed around him, an exhilarating caress of cold, velvety fingers, he relaxed against Shahin and allowed himself a moment of sensory joy. The young man rode through lone back roads for a while before turning onto a narrow dirt path in the middle of an open field. Cai, a bit perplexed about where they might be heading, lifted his head to look around. Darkness was falling already, the autumn night arriving early as usual and lending everything a certain tone of surreal beauty and mystery. When Shahin stopped the motorcycle literally in the middle of nowhere, Cai had a moment of doubt and fear. *What the hell are we doing here?* Was his companion planning something criminal? Was this just an elaborate plan to mug and possibly murder him? Cai shook his head, dismissing his ridiculously fanciful thoughts as he removed the helmet.

Shahin jumped off the motorcycle and stretched like a cat. "Isn't this gorgeous?"

Still confused, Cai stared out into the field stretching before them and blinked. It was dark enough that he couldn't really discern anything of any interest. He was just about to tell the other man that when light flooded everything around them. Straight lines of flickering white lights traced their way through the field as far as the eye could see. An airfield. They were standing at the end of an airfield. Shahin was right. The tarmac seemed to have been graced by the touch of a thousand fairies.

"It's beautiful," Cai whispered in awe.

Shahin returned to the motorcycle and removed a blanket from its small trunk. "Let's get comfortable." He spread it over the grass and sat on it, stretching his long legs in front of him and leaning backward on his arms. "Gorgeous, right?"

Cai joined him on the blanket, still in awe. It was cold, but there was a warmth growing inside him, the kind that always filled him when faced with something of beauty. Distracted by the sight, he didn't notice Shahin's hand inching toward his on the blanket. The touch of his warm fingers startled Cai out of his half-hypnotized state. He sought the other man's eyes and wasn't surprised to find them already staring at him. A flutter of wings inside his chest made him gasp.

Not sure of what to do, Cai closed his fingers around his companion's hand and sighed. "Why the unusual name?"

Shahin chuckled softly. "My mom's idea of a smart play on words. Our flock comes from Spain and our family name means falcon in Spanish, so she looked for a first name that had a similar meaning. A friend of hers was from somewhere in Africa and told her Shahin meant hawk."

"Your name means Hawk Falcon?" Cai laughed. Somehow the name fitted him. There was a sense of the wild in the younger man, something not quite tamed.

Shahin shrugged. "That's my mother for you. Always complicating things that should be simple."

"I like it," Cai said, his voice shrinking to a whisper. "Can I call you Sha?"

The other man's blue eyes glinted like diamonds as he bent over slightly to touch Cai's lips with his. The breath caught in his throat. "Love that you've given me a nickname," Shahin murmured against his lips, sending shivers of pleasure down Cai's spine. "Yes, call me Sha."

It had been a quick, gentle kiss and yet Cai's heart had taken off in a race against itself. Shahin's lips were still tantalizingly close and yet too far. Cai wanted to wrap his arms around the other man's shoulders, pull him against him, and kiss him until they ran out of air. It had been far too long.

WAS IT WEIRD THAT HE thought Cai tasted of fresh air and clouds? He had kissed him lightly and briefly, but the urge to kiss him again was overwhelming. His soul mate's magnetic pull was all-powerful, and it took everything he had not to give in to it. Shahin pulled back from the other man, putting a few extra inches between them, and let out the breath he'd been holding. Cai looked confused—or was it bereft?

"I come here a lot." Small talk seemed to be the way to break the awkward pause following the kiss. Shahin wanted to take it much further, but something told him Cai would be spooked if he came on too strong. So he reined it in, not an easy feat for him.

Cai looked down the runway. "It's beautiful, magical really. But why?"

It was a fair question. The truth was that sitting there at the end of the tarmac, watching small planes taking off and landing, soothed him. It was a poor surrogate for actually flying, but he couldn't take on his hawk form more than a few times a week and when in human form he missed the flying. Painfully. Through the years he had discovered several ways of making up for the temporary lack of wings.

"Not sure," he lied, staring at the handsome man sitting next to him. Cai's face, covered in a light stubble, seemed to shine under the soft light of the moon. "It makes me happy."

Cai turned to him, a smile on his face. "You don't seem the type to enjoy quiet and contemplation."

"Not sure if I should be insulted or flattered." Shahin chuckled. Cai was not wrong. "You'd be surprised by what I enjoy or don't enjoy."

The air had become electric again. Shahin clearly heard the crackle of electricity pop between them as their eyes met and held. Breathing didn't come easily and that pull, that strong pull tightened its hold even more.

"I should go back," Cai said unexpectedly, letting go of his hand and jumping to his feet. "I work early tomorrow and still have to finish some work tonight." Shahin suspected it was merely an excuse, but he was probably right. For once he agreed they should take things slowly. This was not another one of his fly-by-night affairs. Cai was for keeps, whether Shahin liked it or not. And he was not too sure he liked it.

Shahin rode them back to Cai's house, letting out a low protesting groan as the contact between their bodies was broken. He removed his helmet but remained sitting, afraid that if he moved he'd pull the other man into his arms and make a fool out of himself.

Cai handed Shahin his helmet and stared up at the sky as if looking for something. "What are you looking for?" Shahin followed his gaze, but saw nothing more than the darkness of the evening.

"Nothing. It's just—" Cai lowered his gaze to him and smiled. "Dumb really, but I've been followed by a hawk for a while now." Shahin squirmed in his seat. "I know, stupid, right?"

"No, not at all." It was so tempting to tell him. He bit his tongue. "Hawks are smart animals. Did you know they mate for life?" He had never really believed it until he met Cai. Now he was convinced the stories the elders had told the fledglings all their lives were actually true.

Cai shook his head. "I can't say I know much about hawks," he confessed. "They are magnificent, powerful birds, but I never heard of one following a human around. It's bizarre."

"Does it bother you?" He had to know.

"No, it's just a little unsettling. Do you think it would attack me?" Shahin shook his head vigorously. "I mean, they are birds of prey after all."

Shahin shook his head again. "No, it would never attack you. Ever." He may have been a tad too emphatic. Cai looked at him, an eyebrow raised. "I mean, I never heard of a hawk attacking a human."

The other man scratched his head, smoothing the few hairs that stuck up. "I hope you're right." He raised his eyes to Shahin's. "I had fun. Thank you for inviting me, Sha."

The casual use of the nickname made him melt. In one fluid movement, Shahin swung his leg over the cycle and crossed the few feet between them. He held on to Cai's peacoat lapels, pulled him toward him, and covered the other man's lips with his. The heat they produced ran quickly through him, like a tidal wave of desire, making him shiver and tremble. Cai pried Shahin's lips open and caressed him with his tongue. Surprised and incensed by the unexpected heated reaction from serious, timid Cai, he pulled him closer, crashing his hard chest against the other man's. Cai's taste held a promise. Shahin had no clue what his mouth was promising, but he allowed himself to relax against him, enjoying every second of their tongues' sensual dance.

When they pulled apart, their ragged breaths mingling, Shahin was not sure of anything anymore. He was normally the one in control, but his companion had taken over, stunning him by bringing up feelings he was having trouble processing.

"Come over for dinner tomorrow." Cai's whisper surprised Shahin, who still held on to the coat's lapel as if to a lifeline. "I'll cook."

Shahin gulped and nodded, unable to utter a word. Cai smiled and brushed his hand across Shahin's face before turning around and walking into his house. Still stunned, Shahin didn't move for a while, standing on the curb and staring into the empty space where Cai had been just a few moments before. The thought that he could—no, that he *was* his soul mate was still hard to digest. Shahin had always enjoyed his freedom, the long string of lovers with no attachments, no responsibilities, but now he was thinking long-term, forever. It was a very scary idea.

CHAPTER FOUR

SISTERS & OWLS

The smell of burned garlic tickled his nose. Damn! He had been so much into making sure everything was spic and span for Shahin that he had forgotten he had the oil heating up on the stove. Not that he thought Shahin would care whether the house was tidy—the other man did not seem the type at all—but Cai had a tendency to stress over every detail. He ran to the kitchen and slid the pan in the sink and under water. Sizzling steam filled the air.

"Burned dinner already?" Lyra sneaked behind him, stealthy as a ghost. "Are you trying to impress this guy or kill him with fumes?"

Cai took another pan out of the drawer and drizzled some olive oil in it. "Make fun as much as you like, sister." He placed the pot on the stove and proceeded to peel some more garlic. "But may I remind you that you can't cook worth shit? And if it wasn't for me and my amazing culinary skills, you'd never eat a home-cooked meal again.

Lyra laughed and joined him by the butcher block. "Okay, I'll give you that. I do love your cooking." She grabbed the garlic from his hands and began peeling it herself. "You shouldn't be touching garlic before a date. Do you really want to smell that bad?"

He stepped aside and washed his hands under the faucet. "It's not a date." It wasn't—or was it?

"Did you kiss him the last time you saw him?" Lyra smashed the garlic with the chef knife the way her brother had taught her, and then threw it in with the hot oil. The delicious smell of roasted garlic reached his nose, as he took the bowl with the previously chopped onions from the refrigerator.

"Yes, but—"

"Then it's a date." Lyra placed her hands on her hips. "I just don't understand why you invited me. Don't you want to be alone with him?"

God, did he ever. That's why he had invited his sister. He was terrified of being alone with Shahin, of things getting a little too heated for comfort. Not that he didn't want to. Of course, he did. He hadn't been able to sleep the night before thinking of how Shahin's naked body would feel in his arms. How his body would respond to the other man's hard muscles against his own. Yes, it was safer to have a buffer, something or someone who would put the brakes on his unusually intense sexual attraction for this wild creature.

"No, I prefer if things go slowly." It was the truth. At least the truth in his rational mind since his heart and his traitorous body had other ideas. He'd had a few one-night stands since Jack, but he'd never felt this strongly about any of those other men. It had been fun, a welcome release from the daily doldrums, but it was over—completely over—the minute they rolled out of bed and went their separate ways.

With Shahin, things were not that simple. Cai didn't understand why but the fact remained true. He had no wish to get in too deep only to get his heart broken again. The young man gave off the vibes of a wild one, someone who flew from flower to flower, never lingering on any of them particularly, always looking for the next kick, the next thrill. Cai wasn't like that. Cai wanted stability.

"I wish you'd just be willing to have a little fun once in a while, Cai." Lyra took the bowl from his hands and added the onions to the sizzling pan. Cai snatched a wooden spoon from the counter and stirred the wonderfully aromatic mixture. "You're still a young man. You need to enjoy life."

Cai chuckled. "This from the same woman who is always reminding me of how old I'm getting?" He scooped up the cherry tomatoes he'd washed earlier and added them to the pan before stirring again. "You're a funny one, sis."

Lyra stepped behind him and wrapped her arms around her

brother, resting her head on his back. "You know I enjoy teasing you, idiot." *Yes, sometimes a bit too much.* But who was he kidding? Life wouldn't be the same without his sister's sarcastic bite. "I love you, bro. You need to enjoy life a little. Not just work and your art. F-U-N. Do you even know what that is anymore?"

He kept stirring the pan, popping the now soft tomatoes with the back of the spoon. "I do have fun," he protested, not sounding convincing even to his own ears. "I do a lot of things that bring me pleasure."

"Like the skilled hands of a lover?" Cai cringed. He really hated when Lyra mentioned anything sexual to him. It just felt wrong to have his baby sister—even if she was in her late twenties—talk to him about it. "As pleasurable as the warm lips of a lover around—?"

"Oh my God, Lyra. You have no couth whatsoever. Stop!" He tried to cover his ears with his hand, and a piece of onion that had been clinging to the spoon flew across the kitchen. "Please, do not mention any of that when Shahin is here. Promise me."

Lyra dropped her hands and pouted, emulating her younger self. "All right, I promise. You're no fun, Cai."

Cai layered the three different types of fish steaks and sliced potatoes inside the pan, sprinkled everything with salt and pepper, dropped a bay leaf on top, and then poured a mixture of olive oil and fish broth over the whole thing before covering the pan and turning the stove down to low heat. He knew Shahin liked shellfish, but he was hoping he also liked other types of seafood. He had learned to cook this delicious fish stew from a Portuguese chef a few years before, when he had taken some cooking classes in New York. It was now one of his favorite dishes.

"Hand me the bread, please." His sister gave him the baguette he had sliced earlier, and he buttered the slices and slid them into the oven for toasting. Cooking calmed him down almost as well as painting. Maybe it was the fact he had to pay attention to each step, each addition, observing the results like a scientist in a lab. It kept his mind busy and the worries at bay.

The timer on the stove had gone off and the toasted bread was keeping warm in a covered basket when the bell rang. Cai wiped his hands on his pants, worry coming back full force, and stared at the door, paralyzed.

"I'll open it." Lyra skipped to the door, throwing a worried glance at her brother who was still standing motionless in the middle of the kitchen.

The moment Shahin's throaty voice reached his ears his body turned to mush. He swallowed the big knot in his throat and walked into the living room to greet the man who haunted his dreams. Shahin was talking to Lyra, his tall and lean body relaxed and at home in the middle of Cai's living room. Instead, it was Cai who felt out of his element, nervous and anxious about it all. Should he greet him with a kiss? A handshake? A simple "hi"? *Why do I overthink everything?*

In the end, Shahin spared him from a decision. As soon as Cai came close enough, his hand up in greeting, Shahin leaned over and planted a warm kiss on his lips. The snake bite grated against the sensitive skin of Cai's lips, making him shiver with pleasure. Good thing Lyra was there. Things would have taken a turn to the seriously ill-advised otherwise.

Cai cleared his throat and stole a glance at his sister, who was watching him with a telling grin on her face. "I'm glad you came. This is my sister, Lyra."

Shahin turned his head to Lyra and smiled. "I owe you a debt of gratitude," he said. Then he added, winking at Cai, "For being instrumental in us meeting, I mean."

Lyra giggled. "Cai, he's a keeper. Not only is he hot but sweet too." Cai's cheeks burned and he lifted his eyebrows at his impudent sister. But Lyra ignored him, threading her arm through the loop of Shahin's and prodding him gently toward the couch. "So, what are your intentions with my brother?"

"Lyra—"

Shahin laughed, throwing his head back. "No, it's okay, Cai. I like this one." He dropped to the couch with Lyra, their arms still weaved together. "My intentions are to make your brother a very happy man."

Lyra stared at Cai, who had sat next to them and felt as if he was going to spontaneously combust, and grinned. "Then you have my full support. I want my brother to be happy. You might be just the man to do it."

If there was any way he could have dug a hole and hidden inside it, he would have. His sister had taken on their mother's duties as "embarrassment expert" when she had passed away years before. Lyra did it extremely well, even better than their mom.

Shahin laughed again. "You're embarrassing poor Cai," he said, placing a hand on Cai's arm. An electric current ran up his arm and shook him to the core, sending his discomfort flying. "What's for dinner? It smells amazing."

Lyra proved to be an asset during dinner, defusing uncomfortable moments with laughter and allowing Cai moments of unabashed gawking while she distracted the object of his attention. Hours seemed to go by too fast, and soon Shahin announced his imminent departure.

"I've got to go. I promised my mother I'd come over for family time." He laughed softly. "If I don't show up I'll never hear the end of it."

Cai smiled, drinking in the other man's beautiful eyes like a man lost in a desert. "You're lucky you still have a mother. Ours died almost ten years ago."

"Sorry to hear that. What happened?" Shahin crossed his arms, his trademark white T-shirt stretching over his chest muscles.

"Breast cancer." He didn't like to talk about it. Many years had passed, but the pain was still fresh. "It was a long time ago." His voice broke slightly and he lowered his eyes to hide the tears threatening to spill.

Shahin placed a hand on his shoulder, its warmth spreading quickly down Cai's arms and chest. Cai glanced up, swallowing the unshed tears, and smiled.

"I'm so sorry, Cai." He raised his face up and covered Cai's mouth with his. It was a brief and sweet kiss, but his taste lingered on Cai's tongue long after he was gone.

THE ITCH TO FLY WAS strong, but he had promised himself he would keep his human form for the night. He had ridden his black devil to Cai's place and he was going to ride it all the way to his mother's place. Morphing required a change of clothes, which complicated things sometimes. There was also his mother's nagging about the danger of flying at night. She was right of course. There were too many predators abroad in the dark. A hawk may be a powerful bird, but there were even more powerful ones out there.

The family get-together was as always: long and annoying. His mother managed to mention his lack of hatchlings at least three times, garnering a stream of groans from both Shahin and his siblings.

"Mom, really?" Shahin rolled his eyes, painfully aware of how his mother could so easily send him back to his teen years. "There won't be any babies from me. I'm never going to mate with a female."

"But your—plumbing works normally, right?" His sister

groaned and buried her face in her hands. "Then why can't you make a tiny effort and get a girl pregnant? Can't be that complicated."

His brother, Sal, slid an arm over their mother's shoulders and pulled her to him. "Mom, you do understand how these things work, right? Shahin is not going to impregnate a female. Not the regular way, anyway. Stop going on about it. You're making everybody uncomfortable."

His sister's apple pie and his mom's coffee had been the highlight of the evening, as they often were, and by the time he left to go back home, he was as stuffed as a turkey. He stared at his bike and made the last-minute decision to fly instead. He hid his bike behind a bush in the back of the house so his mother wouldn't worry, stripped off his clothes, and stuffed them in the bike's trunk. Standing in the open field, as naked as the day he was hatched, he morphed one inch at a time.

Some shifters hated the process and referred to it as painful or uncomfortable, but Shahin loved the way his body quickly shrank or stretched, how fine hairs thickened and fanned into feathers, how his arms hollowed and turned into a giant span of wings. The softness of his lips hardened and extended into a sharp, fierce beak, and within minutes he was ready to fly the dark skies of night as the red-tailed hawk that lived inside him.

It was a short stretch to his house from there, but hawks didn't see too well at night. He flew a lot slower than his normal speed, afraid of crashing into an electric pole or a taller tree. His full stomach was not helping either, weighing him down and preventing him from flying as high as he should.

Exhaustion and drowsiness conspired against him, and he never saw it until it was too late to avoid it or defend himself.

The great horned owl swooped down on him out of nowhere, sharp talons gripping and puncturing his flesh. The sheer weight of the bird propelled Shahin downward, careening out of control toward the rocky ground below. He didn't have time to register the searing pain across his chest and ribs as the owl's talons tightened around him. His only chance for survival was to morph back into his human form before the owl managed to ground him and tear into his flesh with his sharp beak. Shahin looked around him, looking for a safe place to drop in full human form, but couldn't find anything. In the chaos, he had flown over a busy road, with no safe haven in sight.

He fought for control, zigzagging in the air, but the owl was quickly winning the battle. The great wings of his attacker flapped and curled, hitting him with the power of a whip. He was losing hold on consciousness as the owl's razor-sharp talons dug deeper into his flesh, nails into a quickly closing coffin. From the corner of his eye, he spotted a familiar place—Cai's house. Without hesitation, he gathered the little energy he had left and steered toward it. As he began the shift into human form, the ground approached at dizzying speed, too fast and too solid for comfort. He braced himself for impact. The owl released him as soon as his body became too big and too heavy for it. Shahin gathered momentum and collided with the hard ground, sending a big cloud of feathers and leaves into the air.

Shahin couldn't breathe. He looked at his body and saw blood. A lot of blood. His legs buckled under him when he tried to stand up, so he dragged himself toward Cai's walkway. He was losing strength quickly, and there were still a few feet to the front door. *I'm not going to make it.*

The world wavered in front of his eyes and everything went dark.

CHAPTER FIVE

BLEEDING LOVE

Water cascaded from the wide faucet into the bathtub, releasing clouds of steam and muffling all other sound. Normally he would already be in bed, since he had to get up early the next morning to go to work, but after dinner with his sister and the wild Shahin he felt wide awake. His body vibrated inside and out, unable to shake the feelings the other man stirred in him. Cai sat on the edge of the tub, fully clothed, watching the water slowly fill up the deep basin, mind lost in thought as the bathroom filled with hot mist.

A faint knock woke him up from his reverie. Had he really heard a sound or was he just imagining it? He stood up and opened the door of the bathroom, but he couldn't hear anything. The bathtub was now almost full. He turned off the water and walked out to his linen closet to pick up a clean towel. He heard it again—a definite knock coming from the front door. Was that the neighbor's cat again? Mr. Snuggles often tried to be invited into Cai's house. He suspected the poor cat was terrorized by its five-year-old owner and needed an escape.

"Not tonight, cat." Reluctantly Cai walked down the stairs to his front door, ready to shoo the unwelcome visitor. "I'm looking forward to a long, relaxing bath."

His hand was already on the handle when he heard it again, a scratch rather than a knock and a mumble—a very human sound. Cautiously he looked through the peephole, but couldn't see anything but the empty walkway. Another moan from the door made the decision for him. Slowly, and bracing himself for whatever it might be behind it, he cracked the door open. At first, he didn't see anything, but then he heard another sound coming from the ground. His heart must have hiccupped, because it became very hard to breathe. Lying on the floor in front of the door, in the fetal position with one hand stretched toward the door, was a very beautiful and very naked Shahin.

Paralysis took over his senses and body. What the hell? Why would Shahin be there that late at night, naked and—unconscious? Belatedly he realized that the other man was not moving, his breathing barely noticeable, lying facedown in a puddle. *Shit! That's blood.*

Jumping into action, Cai checked Shahin for a pulse. With a

sigh, he confirmed he was alive. "Shahin, can you hear me?" He gently shook the other man, but he didn't budge. Hesitantly, Cai took hold of Shahin's underarms and dragged him inside as carefully as he could. The unconscious body of his friend left a trail of blood in its wake. Cai didn't have time to worry about it. He wanted to bring Shahin into the relative safety and warmth of his home. He had obviously been attacked.

Once he had brought him into the middle of his living room, Cai locked the front door and returned to Shahin's side, rolling him slowly onto his back. The man was turning a sickly shade of blue as his body temperature dropped, blood spilling out of him. Two deep gashes sliced his abdomen and another long, but shallower cut exposed the flesh on his ribs, just below the pectoral muscle. The blood pouring out of them carried Shahin's life with it.

Cai grabbed a cushion from the couch and pressed against the wounds, trying to stop the blood flow. With a jolt, he realized he had left his phone upstairs in the bathroom. Not sure whether to run upstairs for the phone or continue to press the cushion against the wounds, Cai's stomach somersaulted. The sickly smell of blood assailed his nose. The other man was still a strange color, so Cai grabbed the throw from the couch and threw it over Shahin's naked body, tucking it in around his chin and shoulders.

"Shahin, can you hear me?" The cushion was quickly soaking up with blood. He made the decision. "I'm going to leave you for a few seconds to go get my phone. Hang on." *Don't die on me, please.*

Reluctantly, Cai ran up the stairs and scrambled to find his phone in his rush to go back to Shahin's side. His heart was racing in his chest, fear settling there like an unwanted anchor. He couldn't lose Shahin. They hadn't known each other for very long, but their connection was so strong, he couldn't envision a life without the younger man in it. The idea of losing him left him breathless.

He dialed 911 on his way down the stairs and followed the directions offered to him by the man at the end of the line. The blood flow had slowed down quite a bit, but Shahin was still hemorrhaging, color fading more and more from his cheeks as he struggled for air. The luscious lips he had kissed with such hunger were cold and almost blue when he began performing CPR. Life was oozing out of Shahin and Cai seemed helpless against it.

Tears of panic and pain rolled down his cheeks as he lowered his lips down on Shahin's again for another breath of life. He lingered just above them, the salty drops dripping between them. A sob escaped him. He was going to lose the one person who'd managed to wake him up inside again.

"Strange time to steal a kiss, don't you think?" The voice was weak and hoarse but reached Cai's ears like a burst of angelic music.

"You're alive." Cai caressed the other man's face, wiping his own tears from Shahin's skin.

"Of course I am. Not that easy to kill an Halcón." A faint

chuckle followed his words. "How bad is it?"

Cai had so many questions. What had happened exactly? Why was he naked and bleeding at his door? Why did he have gray feathers stuck in his hair? They would have to wait for later. Cai could hear the sirens approaching. "The ambulance should be here soon."

"Shit. It's going to be hard to explain this." Shahin tried to sit up, but Cai held him down. "I'm fucking naked, Cai. How am I going to explain that to the EMTs? We were having sex when my boyfriend went berserk and scratched me like a cat on speed?"

He had a point. As curious as Cai was about the same thing, he could see how hard it would be to explain the unusual circumstances. "I'll get you some clothes."

Cai helped Shahin into a pair of soft joggers, trembling as his hands brushed against bare skin. Embarrassed for being turned on while the other man lay seriously wounded, Cai lowered his eyes as he pulled the pants over Shahin's narrow hips up to his waist. "How's this?"

"Pity I'm bleeding half to death the first time you see me naked," Shahin whispered, the wild streak back in his eyes. "I'm a lot sexier without all the scratches."

You're plenty sexy right now. Strange that he kept referring to his injuries as scratches. What could have done such a thing? Cai had assumed they were knife cuts, but now that Shahin had said that he wondered—the cuts were pretty jagged, as if the skin and flesh had been torn rather than sliced.

He had no time to ask the question though. The sounds of the sirens were now just outside the door and soon there was knocking. Cai left Shahin's side to open the door to the rescue workers and watched from the sidelines as they proceeded to do their job. When they finally carried Shahin on a stretcher across the threshold, Cai followed without hesitation. It was then Cai realized he would always follow that man, no matter where his path would take him. As weird as it sounded, Cai knew he was deeply and irreversibly in love with Shahin.

THE PAIN HAD FADED TO a dull throbbing around his ribs and belly. The scratches on his side were not deep. Shahin had felt them with his fingers and he knew them to be mostly superficial. They would heal quickly. The ones on his abdomen were a different matter. His fingers had gone in at least a half inch before he felt woozy and removed them. The owl had done a number on him, digging its sharp talons into his flesh. How was he going to explain this to the medical staff? *I was attacked by a psychotic owl?* Somehow, he didn't think people would believe him. In spite of the pain, he laughed under his breath.

"What are you laughing about?" Cai's worried voice was a gentle caress to his tired and sore senses. "I don't find anything funny about this situation."

Shahin reached out to take Cai's hand in his. "Sorry," he whispered, relishing the other man's warmth. "I was just thinking how difficult it's going to be to explain this whole thing to the doctors."

Cai frowned, wrinkles gathering around his eyes. "I would love to hear the story myself."

Cringing, Shahin squeezed Cai's hand in his. "I promise I'll tell you the whole sordid story when we're alone." It was a decision he had just come to. As afraid as he was of what Cai's reaction might be, he had to tell him the truth sooner or later. Cai was his soul mate and Shahin needed him to accept his crazy and unbelievable reality. It would be the first time that he brought an outsider in. "Thank you for being there for me, Cai."

Surprising him, Cai bent down over the stretcher and kissed him, his lips sliding over and bringing warmth back to Shahin's. "I thought I'd lost you." Cai's words blew over his lips in a whisper. "Don't ever do that again."

Shahin grabbed hold of Cai's soft T-shirt and pulled him to his lips, hungry to taste him again. He was addictive. Every time he sampled Cai's exquisite taste, he wanted more. And more. It made him feel as alive as when he flew high above the world, his great wings flapping against the wind, his human limitations left behind. When he kissed Cai he flew even higher. As he lifted himself from the stretcher, a sharp pain in his gut reminded him of his wound. He let go of the other man, who stared at him, breathless and dazed.

"Hey, lovebirds," the EMT in the ambulance with them said. "Can you please leave the loving for later? Like when he's not bleeding to death."

They both looked in the man's direction as if just then realizing his presence. "I'm not really bleeding to death." Ever argumentative, Shahin had to clarify it. "Am I?"

The EMT laughed. "Maybe not. But let's take it easy until we can stitch you up, okay?"

Cai nodded as if the comment was directed at him. "Sorry. Of course, he shouldn't be—" A deep crimson hue invaded his handsome face.

"Aroused?" Shahin loved when his soul mate blushed, his whole body responding to it as if the man had just removed his clothes. "Too late for that." His raucous laughter made him yelp in pain and Cai bent down to him, fear in his eyes. "I'm fine. Serves me right for teasing you."

The ambulance stopped and the EMTs got into action, preventing their conversation from going any further. Wrapped in a whirl of activity, Shahin lost sight of Cai for a few moments and was surprised by the panic that took hold of him. He couldn't breathe. Clutching at his chest, he called Cai's name.

"I'm here, Shahin." The beloved voice soothed his nerves even though he couldn't see him. "I'm right behind you."

"Are you family?" a strange voice asked from behind the stretcher. "Only family members can come in."

Panic rose in his throat again. "He's my husband." The lie surprised even him. Husband? Where had that come from?

Shahin heard Cai cough as if he was choking on something and he smiled. Poor Cai. He didn't seem to be able to handle deception very well.

"I need some information on his health insurance, then, Mr.——?" Shahin heard Cai cough again and whisper his last name.

"I have no insurance," Shahin said, sparing Cai from further questions he couldn't possibly answer. "I'm responsible for all medical expenses."

"I'll need some signatures." The nurse was relentless; like a dog with a bone she wasn't going to let go of.

"Can you please let the medical team treat my husband first? He's bleeding heavily. I'll take care of everything as soon as I know he's safe." The vehemence in Cai's tone shocked and delighted Shahin. The placid, gentle man could be as forceful as the next man, it turned out. "He needs help."

The nurse mumbled something but didn't persist with the questioning. They had finally arrived at the room, and the medical team was in a frenzy of movement. From between a couple of white-robed people he caught a glimpse of Cai, standing in a corner of the small room, arms crossed and eyes trained on him. Shahin gave him what he hoped was a comforting smile, but he couldn't even be sure the other man saw it. There were people everywhere as they prodded, stared at, and discussed his wound.

"We'll have to clean the wound first," one young man said to no one in particular. "There is some debris in it. Then we'll have to stitch it up. What exactly caused these wounds? They're deep and asymmetric."

Shahin stared at him, biting down on his lip. "Are you talking to me? Because that's the first time anyone has actually addressed the man bleeding on the stretcher." The sarcasm in his voice made the man in white cringe a little. "An animal with sharp claws."

The room went quiet as everyone stared down at him, their thoughts so obvious Shahin could almost hear them. They thought he was either full of shit or bonkers.

"Seriously, sir." The same young doctor addressed him again. "We need to know whether it was a criminal act. Do we need to call the police?"

Let them think he was crazy. "Unless you can arrest an owl, then no. It wasn't criminal." He spotted Cai hiding a smile behind his hand. "Can we just get on with it, please? I would really like to keep some of my blood."

Everyone was quiet for a few more seconds and then the rustle of hospital work restarted. A nurse meticulously flushed the wound with saline and tweezed out bits and pieces of what the owl's dirty talons had left behind. Another woman came forward with a syringe and gifted him with an appreciative look before proceeding to slide a needle into his abdomen. He cringed as the anesthesia entered his muscle tissue, spreading like fire. He was not unfamiliar with pain but that didn't mean he liked it. A few more shots followed the first, following the perimeter of the jagged opening of the wounds, each one burning a little less as the numbness began to take hold and stretch across his lower body.

Within a few minutes, he was numb and ready for sutures. The loss of blood and the trauma were getting the best of him. His eyes hid behind lead-heavy lids. Shahin could hear everything going on around him, but he couldn't open his eyes or lift his arms. His body had become so heavy he was afraid he would go through the stretcher into the floor below and keep going until he reached the center of the earth. Any other time that would have sounded ludicrous to him, but at that moment it sounded perfectly rational. He moaned, incapable of actual words. The heat of a hand met his shoulder and held him down gently.

"He's shaking." Cai's voice. Sweet, beautiful Cai. He moaned again. "Something is wrong. Why is he shivering so much?"

"Reaction to the anesthesia. He'll be fine."

Warmth covered his body from head to toe as the nurses stacked heated blankets over him, but the shaking wouldn't stop. He was able to open his eyes finally and Cai's gaze met his. Shahin smiled and tried to speak, but his teeth were chattering uncontrollably. From the corner of his eye, he saw a nurse inject something into his arm, and a sudden sense of relief went through him. The shaking subsided and he could move his arms again. The weight was gone.

"Shahin, are you okay?" It was Cai, his gorgeous lips contorted into a worried frown.

"You're still here." Shahin smiled as the whisper left his lips. "I love you, you know." Had he just said what he thought he had? Had he just declared his love for a man he barely knew in the presence of a whole medical team?

Cai laughed nervously. "The anesthesia is having some weird effects on you." *Sure, if you say so.* "They just gave you a shot of Demerol. The shaking has stopped."

"I'll bring you the papers to sign, Mr. Banes," a nurse said. "He'll be ready to leave the hospital very soon. We also need to go over the wound care for the next few days. Your husband will need someone to help him with it."

Husband? Yes, the little white lie he had told the staff. He had never been the domesticated type, but the word sounded heavenly, so—right. The part of him he had never known existed wanted that to be so very true.

"What's that smile for?" Shahin must have been smiling like a fool because Cai was staring at him, eyebrows knitted together in disbelief. "Are you sure you're okay? You're really acting a little—weird."

Cai was still close to the bed, so Shahin clasped his hand over his arm and pulled him closer. "I'm better than ever," he whispered with a wink. "You got me flying higher than ever, sweet Cai." The other man blushed a bright red, but didn't try to free his hand. "I like it. I like it a lot."

WHAT DID I GET MYSELF *into?* Cai stole a glance toward the man that had captured his heart while he signed his release from the hospital. His new status as Shahin's husband had earned him the right and responsibility to watch over that wild creature, something he was not sure how to feel about. Shahin was a few steps away from him, fussing with a nurse about the fact he was being rolled out of the hospital in a wheelchair. Cai shook his head and returned his attention to the papers in front of him.

"I'm perfectly capable of walking out of this germ-infested hole, thank you very much." The nurse sighed and gave Shahin a look that could melt rock. "Don't look at me like that, lady. My mother has a lot more authority over me, but even she has no luck telling me what to do."

Cai put the papers down and turned to Shahin. "Will you stop fussing already? It's hospital policy. Let them do it." To his surprise, Shahin stopped fighting the nurse and looked up at him with an expression resembling that of a chided child. Cai almost laughed. *I suppose I still got it.* He'd used that voice so many times on his sister when they were younger.

The nurse rolled a subdued Shahin through the hospital hallways up to the front doors, where a taxi waited for them. She held on to the chair while Cai helped the other man into the backseat of the cab. "Good luck with that one," she mumbled under her breath, and wheeled the chair away from them as fast as she could.

Cai chuckled under his breath, closed the car door, and went around to the other side to slide in beside Shahin. "You're not very good at making friends, are you?" Shahin struggled with the seat belt, obviously trying to pretend he was not in any pain. They had kept him in the hospital overnight after assessing him as an "at-risk" patient. All that meant was the doctors were afraid he would somehow tear his stitches as soon as he left the building.

"Where to?" asked the taxi driver.

Hell, I don't know. Cai turned to Shahin, a question in his eyes. Where should he take him? He was supposed to keep an eye on the injured man, but did that mean he should take him home with him? The idea of sharing the same roof with Shahin, the man who had haunted his nights for weeks now, was just as frightening as exciting. He was injured though. It wasn't as if they could—

He stopped his own thoughts, shook his head and said, "I have a guest room you can stay in." Try as he might, his eyes wouldn't meet Shahin's. He was sure the other man was enjoying his discomfort.

"That will be great." If Cai hadn't been sitting, he would have fallen. He'd fully expected Shahin to fight him on this just like he had fought every nurse in the hospital. "Can't imagine a better way to spend the next few days." Cai couldn't be sure he was serious, so he made himself look in his eyes. His deep oceans were calm and almost wistful. He was telling the truth.

Cai gave the driver his address and leaned back on the fake leather seat, breathing a little too fast for someone who was resting. The idea of having Shahin all to himself for a few days was overwhelming. He hadn't had a man stay over since his breakup, much less for an extended period. Of course, Shahin was not just any man, which in itself was even scarier. He had grown so attached to this stranger in such a short time. It was insane and so against everything he had ever believed. Where was his caution? Where was his common sense?

The hospital was not far from his house. After helping a cranky Shahin out of the car and paying for the ride, Cai took a deep breath and headed for the door. "I hope you'll be comfortable here. If you want we can drive to your place later for clothes." He knew he was prattling on for the sake of breaking the awkwardness he felt inside.

"I don't think I'll need any clothes." Cai tripped over the hallway runner and almost fell. Shahin laughed. "Relax. I thought I could borrow some of yours."

Cai's face burned as if he had stuck his head in a hot oven. The handsome devil next to him was having a good time unsettling him.

He knew exactly how to affect Cai in ways no one else ever had. "You're lucky you're injured," Cai surprised himself by saying, "or I may be tempted to hurt you right now."

Shahin did a double take, his mouth dropping open. "Mr. Bane, I am shocked! Never thought you had it in you!"

Cai blushed further but smiled, satisfied with the reaction. "Well, you don't know the half of it."

"But I can't wait to find out." And there it was, the low suggestive voice full of promises that made him shiver from head to toe.

Cai took Shahin to his guest room, which luckily was on the first floor. The man was not well enough to be climbing stairs. His sister stayed over sometimes when her boyfriend was out of town. They had been having movie marathon nights since their mother had died, their own humble way of honoring her love for the big screen. As soon as Zack was out the door, Lyra packed a bag and settled herself in the guest room while he prepared obscene amounts of calorie-laden buttery popcorn to go with whatever movies they'd be watching.

In spite of his bravado, Shahin was visibly tired, pale and hunching slightly. "Why don't you get yourself comfortable," Cai said, worried that his friend was overdoing it. "I'll get you some hot coffee and a pair of pajamas."

On the way to his room, he stopped to drop a K-cup in the coffee machine. Upstairs everything was the same as usual, but it somehow felt different now that Shahin was under the same roof. It was ridiculous, he knew, but nevertheless true. He picked up a newer pair of pajamas from his dresser, a couple towels, and an extra blanket before heading downstairs. His heart hadn't slowed down since they had left the hospital. *I need a cup of coffee too.*

Behind the half-open door of the guest room, Cai tripped over discarded clothes and shoes. Shahin was fast asleep, his bandaged bare chest rising rhythmically with his breath, sheets and blanket pulled barely over his hips, too revealing for Cai's peace of mind. Yet he couldn't take his eyes from the handsome man in his guest bed, his strong hairless chest thinning down to well-defined abs. With his heart racing again, he made himself back away from the room, closing the door behind him and leaving his soul behind.

The phone rang, snapping him out of the half-trance he was in. The ringtone told him it was Lyra and for once he was tempted to ignore the call. *Damn, I wish I didn't love the brat so much.* He picked up.

"Did you pick him up?" Of course, she would want to know. She kept showing an unyielding interest in his relationship with Shahin. "Are you going to see him soon?"

I'm going to regret this. But in reality, he needed to share it with someone even if it was with his increasingly annoying sister. "He's staying at my place." He heard her squeal of delight and smiled. He could never be annoyed at her for long. "I'm supposed to change his dressings every day, so it's just easier if he stays close."

"Of course. The fact that he is hotter than the sun is just a fringe benefit." She laughed at her own joke. "And what exactly do you know about changing bandages? Since when did you become a medical expert?"

"The doctors taught me how at the hospital. They needed someone to do it and I offered." He knew the next question was coming. Lyra was flighty but not stupid. Not by a long shot.

"Why would they do that? Doesn't he have a family?"

He cleared his throat, bracing himself for her reaction. "Shahin told the staff I was his husband."

There was silence from the other end of the line. Cai could hear his sister's breathing, strong and steady. Where was the usual overreaction? The squealing and hooting? The friendly but relentless teasing?

"Excuse me." She was almost whispering, and he could see her in his mind, squinting at the phone. "I must have heard wrong, but I thought you said he told people you were his husband."

Cai swallowed a big knot that had formed in his throat. "I did. He did."

Laughter exploded in his ear. That was more like it. "Oh my God, bro. You guys might as well tie the knot now and get it over with."

"It was just a little white lie. He didn't want his mother to know—" Flustered, he realized he was justifying it to himself as much as to his sister. Was he making excuses for the fact that deep down inside he liked being called Shahin's husband, and having him close even more? He shook his head, annoyed with himself.

"Look, Cai. I'm very happy for you. Shahin has the perfect body to warm that cold bed of yours." Cai was about to protest when her voice switched from teasing to the tender tone he knew she saved for special occasions. "And your heart. He seems like the right one to heal and warm your heart again."

He was quiet for a moment. Yes, that lovely man in the guest room had a knack for making him feel things he hadn't felt in a very long time. And wish for things he had never thought he'd want again.

CHAPTER SIX

SCRAMBLED EGGS & REVELATIONS

He's so cute, the way he blushes every time he sees me without a shirt. Shahin smiled, enjoying the effect he had on his soul mate. He couldn't wait to find out how Cai would react when they made love. Because there would be love to be made in their near future. He could feel it in his bones. A shiver of pleasure ran through him, and he had the sudden urge to morph into his hawk and fly to release all that pent-up energy and longing. But he couldn't. He shouldn't. Not while he was staying with Cai.

Cai had just arrived from work and immediately started fussing about, noticeably flustered by the fact Shahin was walking around bare-chested. The wound on his abdomen was tender and burned at every move, but the pain was nothing compared to the ache he felt in his soul, the craving for his soul mate. There was such need inside him, it scared him sometimes.

"I saw some of your paintings." Cai's head snapped up. His gorgeous green eyes widened, brow furrowed. "They're beautiful."

"Those are private." Cai's voice had gone down to a mumble, the friendly smile of a moment ago gone and replaced by a frown. "You shouldn't have."

Regret and shame were not familiar feelings for Shahin. He had morals and liked to think that as far as empathy went, he was as good at it as the next man, but at that moment he felt unusually heavy with guilt and embarrassment. Somehow he had crossed a forbidden boundary and hurt his soul mate. For the first time in his life, he wanted to go back in time and undo it, ask for permission first. This was obviously something very personal and important to Cai.

"I'm such a dick sometimes, Cai." He wanted to reach out to the other man and hold him, but he knew Cai wouldn't welcome it. Not then. "I'm so sorry. You're right, I shouldn't have. I was curious about you and began snooping around. I'm so sorry."

Cai was quiet, his lips set in a tight line and eyes hidden behind semiclosed eyelids. His breathing was shallow and his shoulders drooped as if the weight of the world had suddenly fallen on them. Shahin wanted to draw Cai into his arms and comfort him. He didn't understand why he would be this hurt about something so innocuous, but he knew Cai well enough now to realize there had to be a very good reason. He had inadvertently touched a sensitive chord.

"I need a moment," Cai said before turning around and heading upstairs to his room.

Shahin heard the door close, and then silence enveloped the room in an uncomfortable sheet of thorns. What had he done? Things had been going so well between the two. A bit too slowly for his taste, but still—there had been progress in the way Cai acted around him. Even his drug-induced—albeit heartfelt—blurted declaration of love hadn't sent the handsome man running. And now this—his lack of impulse control struck out.

Pacing the main floor of the townhouse didn't seem to calm him down and flying while injured was not an option. His eyes kept roving upstairs, but Cai stayed in his room for most of the evening. Anxious and angry at himself, Shahin explored the kitchen. Maybe if he cooked Cai a good meal, he'd be forgiven. The problem was he had never been a good cook. The hawk in him was not too picky about the food he ingested, so often—and mostly because cooking seemed to be such a waste of time—he'd just prepare himself some steak tartare. He doubted that Cai would be such a big fan of raw meat.

"Eggs," he recited to himself, inventorying the contents of the fridge. "Spinach, onions, and cheese. I can do this."

He remembered his sister, the best cook in the family, performing culinary miracles with just a few eggs and whatever was left in the cooler. Determined to figure it out, he fished a couple bowls from the cabinets and got down to work. He laughed under his breath, knowing too well he had no idea what he was doing. After some chopping and whipping, he poured the whole mixture into a large frying pan. A cloud of steam hit him straight in the face and his eyes teared up. He stirred the mixture, wondering if it was normal that the eggs were so runny. He took the pan off the heat and poured its contents on a plate.

"Fuck. That looks like shit." He eyed the rather anemic egg concoction spreading across the white plate like a pile of soggy dog puke.

"It sure does." Cai's voice startled him. He turned around to face the man he loved, his lower lip pinned between his teeth. "What did you kill?"

Cai was wearing a pair of soft gray joggers and a white Henley that clung to his muscled chest. Barefoot, his vertiginous height filling the kitchen doorway, he looked like a god. One that Shahin would very much like to make his.

"I wanted to cook you dinner," Shahin said, glancing over the culinary disaster with disgust. "Obviously I'm not to be trusted around food."

Shahin was still looking at the food and didn't know Cai had crossed the distance between them until he slid his long arms around him and pulled a startled Shahin against him. "I think it was very sweet of you to do that."

Their bodies touched, and Shahin squirmed closer still, elated to discover Cai swelling against him. "It's crap. I'm afraid that the only thing I can prepare is steak tartare." Why was he still talking about food when that was the farthest thing from his mind right then? He wanted to rip that Henley off Cai and sample that hard goodness with his hands and his lips.

"I love steak tartare." Cai's whispered admission surprised him enough that for a moment he forgot he was wrapped in the strong arms of his soul mate. "I'm sorry I made such a big deal about you seeing my paintings."

Shahin's glance wandered to Cai's mouth. "I'm the one who's sorry," Shahin said, unable to take his eyes from Cai's inviting lips. "I should not have pried. I'm sure you have a great reason for not wanting anyone to see them—"

He couldn't finish the sentence. Cai's mouth covered his in a soft kiss that sent a heatwave all the way to his toes. He pulled him closer and moaned against his warm lips. He wanted more.

But Cai had already pulled away, a teasing smile dancing in his eyes. "I think we better order out," he said, nodding toward the unfortunate eggs.

Shahin laughed. "Yes, it's probably a good idea. Pizza?"

They ate pizza on paper plates in the living room, telling each other stories about their families and laughing the evening away. Shahin marveled at the simplicity of it all and how wonderful it made him feel.

"Your family cannot possibly be as kooky as you make it sound." Shahin had shared his mom's crazy fixation with his progeny and how nothing he said made her give up on the idea.

"You have no idea. What do you call a family of about twenty people, including uncles, aunts, and cousins, all living under the same roof?" He laughed and wiped his lips with a napkin. "The house is like a fucking chicken coop minus the eggs."

"I have my sister, Lyra, who I swear can make just as much noise as all your family put together." Cai smiled, his eyes softening as he talked about his sister. "She can be a serious kook."

"I hope you don't mind me asking, but what happened to your dad?" Cai often mentioned his mom's passing, but his father always seemed to be kept out of the conversation.

Cai sobered and cleared his throat. "Nothing really. He just left a few years back. Shortly after Mom passed away. I don't think he knew how to live without her." Cai's forest eyes clouded over. "He calls every once in a while, but hasn't come to visit or asked us to go see him since he left."

Shahin covered Cai's hand with his. "Just left you guys like that?"

A soft chuckle left Cai's lips. "Well, we were both adults already. Not like we needed him to take care of us or anything—it was harder on Lyra, I think. She had always been daddy's girl."

"You stepped in." It was not a question. He had noticed how Cai's whole body softened when he talked about his sister, much like a father talking about his daughter. "She's lucky to have you, Cai. Very lucky."

Cai lowered his eyes and stared at their entwined fingers as if admiring a work of art. "I'm just as lucky to have her."

They sat together for a few moments, hand in hand, eyes locked in silent conversation.

"It's getting late," Cai said suddenly, his hand dropping Shahin's. "We should change your dressing before going to sleep."

Shahin jumped to his feet and immediately regretted the move. "Holy shit, that hurts."

"You go get comfortable and I'll go get the medical supplies. They're upstairs in my bathroom."

Cai went up, and Shahin walked slowly to the guest room, holding on to his side. Good thing he was a quick healer. In a week or so the doctors were going to be really surprised when he came for his checkup and all that was left of the wound was a well-healed scar. He took off his shirt and for once folded it on top of the armchair instead of throwing it in the corner. Cai's tidiness was rubbing off on him. He climbed on top of the bed and leaned back on the pillows, the pain radiating from his abdomen to his chest and his back.

"You really need to take it easy, Sha." A shiver ran through him as it always did when Cai called him by his nickname. "Those cuts were pretty deep." He walked into the bedroom, several items in his hands. "Which brings me to my next question—what in heaven's name did that to you?"

Shahin wanted to tell him, but he was terrified. Who would blame Cai for running once he found out Shahin was a shifter? It wasn't like confessing you had a weird obsession with Christmas trees. He had been born to a family of shifters and even he had freaked out the day he found out his hands could turn into talons and his bones could become hollow. It was the stuff of fiction, of fantasy novels, not of real life.

"You wouldn't believe me." Lame excuse, he knew. "Can we do this first? It's bothering me." Not a total lie since the wound was hurting, the stitches pulling on his quickly healing flesh.

Cai sprang into action, setting up scissors, bandages, and saline solution syringes on a small towel on top of the nightstand. Shahin began peeling the bandage off, groaning at the discomfort it caused him.

"Will you wait?" Cai sounded annoyed. "Let me do it. You're pulling on the wound." With the deft fingers of an artist, Cai took over, pulling off the sticky bandage with one hand and pressing gently over it with the other hand, so it wouldn't tug on the sensitive skin of the laceration itself. "Are you always like this?"

Cai had his eyes trained on what he was doing, and Shahin's gaze followed his fingers with interest. "Like what? Charming and sweet?"

The silver head turned and green met Shahin's eyes. "Right." He chuckled and turned his attention back to the bandages. "Impulsive and reckless?"

Shahin tried to infuse his voice with outrage. "What makes you think I'm reckless, pray tell?" The removal of his dressing was painless, Cai taking his time to peel it back inch by inch.

"Well, you did show up naked and bloody at my door in the middle of the night." His voice caught on the word naked and Shahin smiled.

"My family has strange mating rituals." Again, not exactly a lie. He laughed. "I thought you'd go for that kind of thing."

"Bloody and half-dead? Yes, very sexy indeed." Cai snickered. "Are you ever going to tell me exactly what happened? Was it something illegal?" He had finished removing the bandage and stared at Shahin.

"I promise I'm a law-abiding man. Nothing illegal was going on." Shahin watched Cai as he placed the bloody gauze on the towel, picked up a syringe, and turned back to him. "That looks ominous." He'd never had much love for needles.

Cai laughed and waved the syringe in front of him. "There isn't a needle in this thing. It's a squirter. It squirts saline solution." He demonstrated by pressing the plunger and spraying liquid into the air. "See?"

It was mesmerizing to see him cleaning the wound, the saline flow leaving a pleasant cool feeling behind as it dripped off the sides of his belly and chest. Cai sat down on the edge of the bed and soaked the excess liquid with a piece of gauze before covering the injury with a self-sticking bandage. As he eased the edges with gentle fingers, Shahin's skin tingled under his touch, his muscles contracting in pleasure.

Cai's movements slowed down, his fingers lingering longer than necessary over Shahin's abs, his eyes never coming out from behind his lashes. "We probably should do something about that scratch too." It was almost a whisper, deep and raspy as if he was having trouble talking.

His hand moved to the long but shallow gash on Shahin's chest, tracing it with feathery fingers, a maddening caress that set Shahin on fire. A quiet moan escaped his lips as Cai bent down and followed his fingers with his lips, peppering it with a line of slow kisses. Shahin threw his head backward into the pillows with a grunt.

Cai's lips continued their journey upward over his chest, then his neck. He lingered over the rose tattoo. "I've been wanting to touch these since I first saw you." He nuzzled the crook of his neck as Shahin spread his hand around Cai's neck and pulled him closer.

The fire inside Shahin had grown into a monster that demanded to be fed. He tried to sit up, but Cai pushed him down on the pillows and climbed onto the bed, straddling him in one fluid motion. "Stop me if I'm hurting you."

Cai's lower body hovered tantalizingly over Shahin's but didn't touch it. Shahin wanted to feel his weight on him, his heat against his. "I want you, Cai."

Breath coming out in spurts, Cai shook his head. "You're injured.

We shouldn't."

"Fuck the injury," Shahin exclaimed, holding Cai by the waist and pulling him down on him. "We're doing this."

WITH SHAHIN SWELLING AGAINST HIM, Cai was close to losing control. He wanted this man more than anything he'd ever wanted before. But he was injured, and any strenuous activity might open his stitches. Cai was used to being the sensible one, the one who always did the right thing. But having Shahin under him, vulnerable and inviting, felt so right—would it be the wrong thing to do?

"Shit, Shahin, we have to stop." His brain was telling him he needed to put some space between them, but his heart and his body didn't agree. "You're hurt. You'll bleed to death."

Shahin laughed, and Cai's body surrendered to his soul mate's pressure. "I'm a fast healer. I'll be fine." Cai shivered as Shahin slid his hands under his shirt and pulled it up just enough to feel the hard muscle beneath. "You feel so good."

Cai sighed and leaned over to the other man. "You're too reckless." He moved forward a few more inches and captured Shahin's mouth with his, tracing the edges of his lips with his tongue. Shahin always tasted of the wild, trees and sky, ocean and clouds. Paradoxically this wildness grounded Cai, soothed the restlessness that seemed to have taken over his usually placid soul. "I love it."

Frantic, Shahin pulled harder on Cai's shirt until it bunched up around his neck. "Get rid of this. Please." There was a tone of desperation in Shahin's voice, longing beyond any Cai had ever experienced before.

He sat up straight and removed the offending item of clothing, throwing it over his head and to the wooden floor by the door. Shahin ran his warm hands over Cai's exposed abs and chest, lingering over his pecs, and playing with the smattering of dark hair that covered it. Cai moaned, a wave of yearning and pleasure washing and taking control over him. A hazy thought about how he needed to stop before Shahin got hurt sang in the back of his mind, too quietly to be fully heard.

Shahin pulled him down again, latching his lips to Cai's in a hungry, demanding kiss. Cai met his searching tongue with his and delighted at the way it felt as it danced with his, savoring him whole. He gasped, surprised by how his body fiercely responded, softness turning into hardness so fast he almost lost control again.

His heart pounded in his chest and in his ears, a ticking bomb about to explode. Shahin reached between them and slid a hand inside Cai's pants. "I want you now."

Cai yelled, shuddering in an earthquake of pleasure. He wanted this. With all his body and soul. But he couldn't allow Shahin's recklessness to infect him with a sense of invulnerability. The man begging to take him was seriously hurt, and making love would almost certainly reopen his wound. Gathering strength and control he didn't know he had, Cai jumped off the bed.

"What the—? What happened?" Shahin turned the palms of his hands up in front of him and shrugged. He pinched his lips together and clenched his jaw, his desire obvious under the thin sheet that covered his lower body.

Cai looked longingly at the gorgeous man in his guest bed, ready and willing, and had a moment of doubt. If they were careful, maybe it wouldn't hurt him. *No, don't be stupid.* He shook his head. "We can't. Not now. Not yet."

Shahin stared at him, blue eyes glittering under the ceiling light. If eyes could talk, those would be cursing him out. Cai shifted uncomfortably, still hard and jittery with desire, and willed himself to smile however awkwardly. It took a few long moments but the other man smiled back. Shahin's smile lit up the room, a smile that started on his lips but spread to his eyes, his cheeks, his whole body. *Irresistible Sha.*

"I think I'll take a cold shower," Cai said, searching for his discarded Henley with his eyes. "You?"

With a wink, Shahin rested back on his pillows. The weight of his arms pulled on both sides of the sheet, allowing Cai a full view of how he affected the wild creature in that bed. "Only if I can take it with you."

Suddenly very self-conscious of his state of undress, Cai grabbed his shirt and slipped it over his shoulders. "The doctors said you needed at least forty-eight hours of complete rest." He hated how he sounded, like an old man correcting a young one.

"I'll set my alarm." The handsome devil seemed to love making him squirm. "I'll be counting the minutes."

Cai groaned, turned his back, and left the room. A smile popped onto his lips as he walked away. *Damn you, Sha, you're relentless and I love it.*

After a very cold shower, Cai was too awake to go to sleep. Afraid of sitting in the living room, too close to the guest room, he sat on his bed, reading a book, his mind constantly wandering to the man downstairs. Images of how deliciously sexy he had looked, half-naked under the sheets and so... ready wouldn't let him focus.

A loud knock on the door wrenched him out of his dangerous thoughts. Who could it be? Cai threw a glance at the clock. It was way past midnight. Suddenly panicky with thoughts of tragic accidents involving his sister, Cai jumped out of bed and ran downstairs to the door. A look through the peephole told him it was no one he had ever met. A short, middle-aged woman stood on the other side of the door, arms crossed and lips pinched into a frown. *Who the hell is this?*

"May I help you?" Cai cracked the door open and looked at the woman through the gap. Behind her on the street, Cai noticed a red minivan, the headlights still on. "Did your car break down?"

She looked him straight in the eye. "So, you're the one."

Confused, Cai stared at her squinting eyes. "Is my son here?"

"Your son? Do I know you?" Cai narrowed his eyes, still holding on to the door.

"Is Shahin here?" *Shahin? How——?* "I'm his mother. Is he here?"

Cai immediately opened the door all the way. "I'm so sorry. I didn't know. Please, come in." He backed away from the doorway to make room for the tiny woman to step inside. "Did something happen?"

He closed the door behind them and invited her toward the sofa, but she didn't move. "Yes, *you* happened. It's all your fault."

What in heaven's name was she talking about? "Excuse me? My fault for what?"

Shahin's mother looked around, searching. "Where is he? Where's my son?"

Cai blinked, still confused. "He's probably asleep. It's after midnight." The woman surveyed him from head to toe. Why was he feeling as if he was standing naked in the middle of the living room? "I'll go check."

Leaving the disgruntled woman in the living room, Cai stepped into the hallway and headed toward the guest room almost directly under the staircase. Before knocking, he put an ear against the door and listened for signs of movement, but could hear none. He knocked gently. "Sha? Are you awake?" Cracking the door open, he cautiously looked inside. The lights were all off, and all he could see was the outline of the furniture. "Sha?"

"Have you changed your mind and you're coming to ravish me?" He never gave up. In spite of the strangeness of the situation with the woman in the living room, Cai chuckled under his breath.

"Your mother is here." Cai thought he heard a sudden intake of air and a thump. Shahin had got out of bed.

"My mom? Are you kidding me?" Shahin's flawless face emerged from the dark. "How did she find out I was here?"

Cai was wondering the same.

The two made their way to the living room, Cai walking a couple steps behind Shahin, who had neglected to put on a shirt. Cai wrapped his robe tighter around himself to hide his immediate reaction to the other man's bare skin.

"Mom! What the hell are you doing here so late?" Shahin exclaimed as soon as they walked in the room. "Why would you wake poor Cai up? He has to go to work early tomorrow."

Mrs. Halcón's eyes moved from her son to Cai and she frowned. "He's the reason, isn't he? *This* is why you refuse to heed my requests?"

Cai was pretty sure he should feel offended by her words, but he couldn't be sure what he was being blamed for.

"Mother, Cai has nothing to do with my refusal to listen to your insane and irrational demands." Shahin crossed his arms and the skin on his chest tightened over his muscles. Cai gulped. "Reality and common sense, Mom, two things you seem to be sorely lacking."

Cai cleared his throat. "I apologize for interrupting, but can someone explain to me what's going on? And what I'm being blamed for?"

Shahin cackled. "My insane mom can't accept the fact that I will never mate with a female and give her little Shahins." Not for the first time, Cai noticed the unusual way Shahin talked sometimes. "Even though she knows very well I prefer the male of the species, she still hopes I will fuck some girl and get her pregnant."

Cai cringed at the use of the F-word in front of Shahin's mother. His own mother would have killed him if he ever had the nerve to use such language when talking to her. Mrs. Halcón didn't even flinch.

"I think I was wearing you down at some point," the woman explained, her lips still stretched into a thin line as she glared at Cai. "But then you showed up." She turned to her son. "He's not even one of us, Shahin. He's not a *cambiador* like us. How will that work?"

Annoyance had replaced Cai's confusion. What were they talking about? "What's a *cambiador*? Can you guys please talk like normal people?"

Shahin's mother looked back at Cai and rolled her eyes. "For God's sake, Shahin. He doesn't know?"

Cai clenched his hands along the side of his body and growled. "I have no freaking clue what you're talking about, but it's the middle of the night and you're driving me crazy. What the hell are you talking about? What don't I know? And why are you so pissed about it?"

The woman looked at her son one more time and then dropped

onto the nearest couch. "He hasn't told you he's a shifter."

He was not sure what he'd expected, but *that* wasn't it. "A shifter? You mean someone who moves around a lot?" Cai stole a glance at Shahin, who had grown quiet and looked at him with apprehension.

"Not a drifter, you fool." The woman was the rudest, most irritating woman he had ever met. "A shifter. Someone who shares a body with an animal."

The words hit and slid off him. "What? That's very funny—" The absurdity of what she was telling him made him burst out laughing. But a quick look at Shahin told him she was not joking. "Shahin? What does this mean?"

The other man, dark and stunning, rubbed the back of his neck in obvious discomfort. "I was going to tell you, but I was waiting for the right time. The right words." His voice had gone quiet. "I'm a shifter. I'm a man and a hawk. I can hold my human shape for a while at a time, but at some point, I have to shift into my hawk shape in order to recharge, to survive."

Cai's chin had dropped and his heart was beating so fast he was afraid it would jump out of his chest and run away on its own. "A hawk?" He was surprised that the idea was not the total shock it should have been. "Are you the hawk that's been following me? The one I talked to you about?"

Shahin nodded and lowered his eyes. "Yes, that was me."

"You've been stalking me?"

Shahin looked up. "I tell you I'm a fucking hawk and all you are worried about is that I was following you?"

"Stalking. The correct term is stalking me." Cai's lowered voice sounded menacing. "You planned this—this... whatever this is."

Cai closed his eyes, trying to shut out the confusion around and inside him. He felt dizzy, nauseous as if he'd been forced into several rides on a roller coaster, not sure of what to feel, what to believe. He wanted to throw up, empty his stomach and his heart, and feel nothing. Why wasn't he mad? Why wasn't he raving at Shahin? *Kick him out. Kick him out.* No matter what his brain was telling him, he couldn't move, couldn't think straight.

He dropped onto the couch, cradling his head with his hands, and willed Shahin and his mother away. Silently. Inefficiently. When he reopened his eyes, they were still there, both staring at him.

Cai looked up at Shahin, pain crushing his chest. "You tricked me into falling for you."

Shahin's eyes popped open. "You fell for me?"

"That's all you got from this conversation? Are you fucking crazy?" Cai was beside himself, disbelief in his tone. "You can stay the night, but you better be gone from my house by the time I come back from work."

Cai turned to the mother who had been listening to the exchange with blatant curiosity and a smile on her face.

"And as for you, Mrs. Halcón, you can sleep at ease because

there is nothing between your son and me and there will never be. Show yourself out." With those words, Cai swiveled on his heels and stomped upstairs, his heart shrinking with the familiar feeling of heartbreak. What a fool he'd been to believe he could love and be loved again.

"Cai, please wait." Shahin ran after him and gripped his arm halfway up the stairs. "You have to let me explain. Please."

A deep mantle of sadness fell over him and swallowed him whole. "There's nothing to explain, Shahin." Cai wanted to bury himself in those soulful blue eyes even now. "I trusted you and you—"

"But I love you, Cai. You're my soul mate."

God, he had wanted to hear those words! But it was too late. He had fallen in love too fast, too deeply. With the wrong person.

CAN HEARTBREAK KILL YOU? SHAHIN could feel his heart actually cracking and shattering into a million pieces. He placed a fisted hand on his chest in an attempt to stop the pain, but it didn't do him any good. How was it possible this could hurt so much? He'd had relationships before, so-called love affairs, but he had never once felt this agony that choked him to tears. Being in love was not half as fun as books and movies made it look like, it turned out. He had never before been in love or believed he would ever be. But that was before Cai, before he discovered the myth of the soul mate was an actual thing. His heart was irreversibly connected to Cai's and the thought that he had inadvertently caused a breakup before they actually started their love story was too painful to bear.

Listen to you, idiot. You sound like a romantic fool. He didn't have a sentimental bone in his body. Or so he had always been told. Had he been wrong all these years? Because he felt pretty sappy at the moment, tears dancing in his eyes, a fierce ache in his heart and soul.

"Go home, Mom." He barely recognized his voice as he turned to face his mother. "You've done enough harm tonight. Go home."

Lips still stretched into a thin line, his mom took a step forward, but he stopped her.

"Don't want to talk to you right now. Go home."

"I know you're mad at me right now, but it was better this way. Your man is not a *cambiador*. Your relationship couldn't go anywhere." His mother spoke softly but firmly. "You could never be a couple."

Shahin snapped his chin up and stared at the woman who called herself his mother. "Do you even know what love is, Mom? I'm in love with that man up there and my heart couldn't care less whether he is a shifter or a plain human. He's my soul mate, Mom. My soul mate." His mother flinched. "Tell me again—what happens if a shifter can't be with his soul mate?"

She cleared her throat. "The shifter won't ever be able to mate with anyone else." Her voice came out as a whisper. Her eyes lowered and her lips finally smoothed out.

"Right. I will never be able to mate with anyone else, Mom." He spat out the words, his eyes shooting bullets. "Not even with your precious female hawks. Go home."

The tiny woman huffed a little and left, slamming the door behind her. Shahin stared at the door for a few moments, looking but not seeing. If he followed his instincts and what his heart was telling him to do, he would run upstairs and burst through Cai's door to tell him how sorry he was. Common sense told him such an action would only solidify Cai's suspicions that he was a stalker.

After stealing a longing glance at the top of the stairs, Shahin retreated to his room, lay down on top of the sheets, and buried his face in the soft pillows. He couldn't remember a time he had actually cried. Surely he had cried as a baby or a toddler, but as far as his memory stretched, there wasn't a single instance of tears other than those caused by laughing too hard. His pillow was the only witness to the tears that spilled from his eyes and rolled down his cheeks that night. This soul mate thing was very real. It felt as if his heart had been yanked out of his chest while still beating, a sense of helplessness and loss taking over his common sense. Life was not over just because the man he lusted over didn't want him. No, that was not true. Not the man he *lusted* over. The man he needed, whom he loved. What had possessed him to follow Cai? He had never snooped into personal moments, just out in the street and mostly from afar, but still—Cai didn't see it that way. What had he done?

The night was a long succession of tosses and turns, staring at the ceiling and groaning into the pillow. By morning he had decided. He'd give Cai the space and time to think things through and then— well, he wasn't sure what he'd do, but he would most definitely do something to try to win his man back. A hawk always mated for life, and he had found the one he wanted to spend the rest of his life with.

CHAPTER SEVEN

HOLDING THE KEY

"**A**re you listening to me, Cai?" Ted was standing beside his desk, arms crossed and brows furrowed.

Cai shook his head, waking himself up from thoughts he'd rather not have. "Sorry, Ted. I'm a little distracted this morning." Understatement of the century. He couldn't focus on anything no matter how hard he tried. "I'm going for a walk to try and wake up."

Grabbing his coat on the way out the door, Cai rushed past his coworkers and down the stairs into the street. The wind greeted him with a strong, frigid slap on the face. He tied his scarf tighter around his neck and stuffed his hands into the coat's pockets before beginning his walk around town. Old Manassas was a quaint little town, with one-way streets lined by old buildings and specialty stores. He loved it here. It filled him with a strange sense of peace, walking down the autumnal streets, the traffic zooming along and people rushing by, trying to get out of the wind.

It had been a hard morning. After a sleepless night, Cai dragged himself out of bed earlier than he had to. He'd showered and got dressed before going down to find the guest room empty. Shahin had left sometime during the night. *He shouldn't have. He's hurt.*

What was he thinking? Why was he fussing over the man who had so obviously stalked him before they even met? What did he care if he was hurt or not? Shahin had stripped the bed and folded the blankets and sheets neatly on a chair. Cai's heart contracted a little at the memory. The room had looked so empty without the young, vibrant man.

Cai touched the metal object inside his pocket, twirling it between his fingers. He had found it that morning in an envelope by the coffee machine, tucked within the fold of a handwritten note. Shahin had beautiful, intricate script handwriting. Every word looked like a tiny piece of art, a sweet-sounding poem inscribed on common paper.

You have the right to be angry at me. I deserve it. I should have not followed you, I agree. But there is more to the story that you don't know, and I wish you'd let me explain to you. When you're ready, come see me. My house is always open for you no matter what time. I love you.

He had left a house key along with the note, the key that Cai now held between his fingers. He was angry. So angry he hadn't even had time to think about the bigger issue—a shifter? Was that even possible? He had heard stories, of course. Mostly fictional narratives for fantasy lovers. But Shahin was the real thing. A man who turned into a hawk and vice versa. Which side of him was the dominant one, and would he have to pick one of them sometime during his lifespan? So many questions and yet, the only ones he really wanted to ask at the moment were "Why were you stalking me? What were you planning?"

Cai walked around the block and realized he was standing by the coffee shop he had taken Shahin to that day a few weeks back. After a moment's hesitation, he went in out of the cold and surveyed the space. The couch where they had sat together was empty and calling him. The girl behind the counter waved at him and mouthed the name of the coffee drink he ordered every day. He thanked her and sat down, caressing the seat beside him, lost in thought. The coarse material scratched against his fingers, a bittersweet reminder of the hawk-man's day-old stubble. He missed him already, and no amount of telling himself Shahin had done something underhanded and disrespectful was going to change that.

Time wove its ever-growing web while he sat quietly, a deep ache and emptiness in his heart. The sound of the eleven o'clock train yanked him from his reverie. What was he doing? He should be working on his current project. The deadline was looming just ahead, and he was wasting his time pining over a man he barely knew. Cai stood up, grabbed his coat, and left. He would have to wait until the evening to grieve a relationship that never was.

Ted walked him to the car after work, his hands stuffed in his pockets and eyes glued to the ground. Cai knew he wanted to say something but hadn't quite found the courage to do it. Taking pity on his old friend, Cai said, "All right, Ted, spit it out. I'm afraid you may explode otherwise."

Ted lifted his hazelnut eyes to his and smiled almost apologetically. "I don't want you to be mad at me."

"Ted, we've been friends for a very long time. If I'm mad at you, I'll tell you." Cai knew that whatever it was his friend was about to say had something to do with Shahin. Ted was not a fan of the young shifter, but then again Cai suspected that even though they hadn't been a couple since they graduated from high school, Ted still harbored lingering feelings for him.

"You have that look you had when Jack left you." Cai cringed. Those were not good memories. "Did something happen with the wild one?"

Cai laughed softly. "The wild one?" It was a pretty fitting nickname for Shahin. "What makes you think something happened?"

His friend brushed a hand over his own face and sighed. "Let's see. You're walking around like a zombie, head in the clouds, and doing that—that thing you do with your lips when you are upset."

"I do a thing?" Cai's voice rose an octave or two, his hand flying to his chest.

"Your mouth slackens and you stare at nothing in particular." Ted mimicked the expression and Cai burst out laughing. "Don't laugh. It's pretty pitiful."

"Okay, maybe something did happen," he admitted, the laughter dying down. "I'm not ready to talk about it yet. I need to sort some things out in my head first. You'll be the first I come to when I'm ready. I promise."

Seemingly satisfied with Cai's promise, Ted nodded and resumed his walk. Cai got into his car and waved at his friend, who was already walking away. He turned the key in the ignition but didn't move out of the parking space. Sliding a hand into his pocket, he removed the key and the note that came with it. Besides the message, there was an address. Shahin's. His fingers caressed the cold key, feeling the roughness of the edges on his skin, the smooth curves, and the hollowed spaces in between. He was tempted. Very tempted to drive over and forget everything he had learned to lose himself in the hawk-man's arms.

Dismissing his fanciful thoughts, Cai put the key away and drove off. He needed time and space to figure things out, to make sense of the craziness that was Shahin. The dazzling, drop-dead gorgeous mess that was the man he'd fallen in love with.

THE STITCHES WERE TIGHT ON his side, making it uncomfortable to move as he slipped into the wingsuit. His wound didn't allow him to change into a hawk. Not yet. The human could handle the wound, but the hawk would most likely perish from it. The owl had done a number on his winged body, tearing it from one side to the other. Had he not morphed into his human form, he would most certainly have died. But he was not going to allow an injury to stop him from the therapeutic benefits of flying. More than ever, he needed to fly. He need to feel the wind buffeting his face, supporting his body as he glided through the air and plummeted toward the ground. Some people drank, some took drugs; he flew. The freedom that flying offered him soothed his aching heart.

Irritated with his own feelings, Shahin zipped up the cumbersome suit and buckled the parachute to his back. Normally he wouldn't need it, but considering that shifting was not an option at the moment, it seemed wise to carry one. What he couldn't protect himself from was the wrenching pain that was tearing him apart. Not that long ago, if anyone had told him he would love someone as much as he loved Cai, he would have laughed in their faces. Shahin didn't attach himself to anyone that way. He was a free agent, a player. He was all about one-night stands and never-ending fun. This attraction he felt for the handsome and levelheaded Cai was inexplicable, an oddity he wanted to deny but couldn't.

Growing up listening to stories about the mythical soul mates whom nobody he knew had actually ever met, he thought those were just that—stories. Hard to believe that he had found his soul mate. Of all shifters, he was the least likely to fall in love, to make the deep, irresistible soul connection—one that once found could not be reversed. His breakup with Cai affected him in ways he had never thought possible.

In one single move, Shahin jumped off the ledge of the mountain and free-fell a few feet before opening his arms and gliding smoothly in downward circles. For a few moments, while suspended high above the ground, Shahin blanked out all thoughts of his soul mate and focused only on the exhilarating thrill of the experience.

Too soon he was on the ground again, gathering the maze of parachute cables, his mind already on a collision course with memories of Cai. Stripping off the heavy wingsuit, he noticed wetness around his middle. Some of the stitches had popped opened. He didn't care. Pain was good. It distracted him from the different kind of pain he had so much more trouble dealing with. After stuffing the wingsuit in the usual hiding place, a hole in the ground behind some trees, he got on his bike and rode it as if he was being chased by a banshee.

Shahin found himself in Old Town Manassas. What used to be simply a small town near his house had become a symbol for so much more, a place he now associated with painful feelings of heart-wrenching longing. His mother and other elders had told him often about the pull of the soul mate. "Once you meet her, your life will be consumed by the need to be close to her. Every time you're apart will be as if your heart is being pulled out of your chest by an owl's sharp talons." He was well acquainted with the feeling now. He'd be doomed to a life of misery if Cai never forgave him. "There is no way to fight it."

Leaving his bike parked by the train station, he walked the few yards across the rails to their coffee shop. Shahin started at his choice of words. "Their," not "the" or "a"—*their* coffee shop. *Shit. I'm so fucked, it's not even funny.*

As he crossed the threshold, his eyes went straight to the spot Cai, and he had sat so many times. The seats were taken by another couple. It took him a few moments to realize one of the men sitting there was Cai. The other one was his coworker and friend, Ted. Shahin's heart took the reins. Crossing the floor in a few wide strides, he went to stand in front of them, jealousy brewing in his chest— and anger so hot, everything he looked at turned slightly red.

"You wasted no time, did you?" The growl came through his clenched jaw. "It's been what? Two days? And you're already buddying up with good old Ted here."

Cai stared at him, uncomprehending at first and then angry, but said nothing. Ted stood up, visibly nervous, and looked at Shahin. "Listen, man. There is nothing romantic between me and Cai. We're just friends."

Shahin ignored him. "Did you run to his bed as soon as I was out of yours?"

The angry exchange was attracting some attention from the other patrons. Cai stood up and gestured for him to follow him to the back, where there were private rooms. "I'll be back, Ted."

He was sure he was fuming, actually letting out smoke through his ears and eyes. Shahin couldn't remember a time when he'd been this angry. Things tended to just slide off him, like water over a raincoat. But he couldn't control the anger, the jealousy he was feeling at the moment. He followed Cai, ignoring the curious stares he was attracting from the other customers.

"You have no right." Cai's voice was infuriatingly steady and calm. "You have absolutely no right to accuse or be angry at me."

Shahin's breath came out in small spurts to match the frantic beat of his heart. "You didn't let me explain myself. I know what I did was not right, but I had a reason, a very good reason."

"I shouldn't even be listening to you." His low tone was maddening. Shahin wanted Cai to rave and yell at him, hit him with angry fists and make him pay for his transgression. He didn't want this calm, collected man who didn't seem affected at all by what had happened. Did he not feel the pull? He had to. The soul mate thing went both ways. "But I confess I'm curious. What possible explanation can you have for your stalker behavior?"

Taking a deep breath, Shahin tried to calm himself down. *Breathe, breathe.* "It's the soul mate pull." As soon as he said it, he knew he wasn't making any sense. Cai looked at him with raised eyebrows. "It's a shifter thing. When you meet your soul mate, the one whose body and soul are cosmically connected to you, there's no way out. You feel a pull, an irresistible urge—no, a need. An irresistible need to be close to your mate. It hurts if you can't. Physically hurts."

Cai guffawed, throwing his head back. "You got to be kidding. This is what you came up with? A myth from a fantasy book? Is this a joke?"

"You must be feeling it too." Shahin's voice had taken on a tone of desperation. "You must. I feel like I'm about to implode, such is the emptiness in me. We belong together, Cai. There's no denying it. The universe wants us together."

"Fuck, Shahin. That's a bunch of horseshit." Shahin cringed, unused to hearing Cai's swearing. "You could at least come up with a better explanation of why you followed me around without my knowledge. Soul mates? The pull of the mate? You sound as if you're quoting from a fantasy book. Fictional, Shahin, all fictional."

Shahin straightened up. "Then how do you explain me being a shifter?" His voice had leveled and lowered, a hint of sadness and resignation to it. "How can you explain how I was attacked by an owl on my way home as a hawk? How do you explain that? Am I also fictional? Did you read me out of a book or create me in your dreams?"

Cai fell silent, his eyes searching Shahin's. Fighting the strong urge to take him in his arms and encouraged by the silence, Shahin smiled weakly.

"I love you. I've never in my life felt like this toward anyone. You're my soul mate and I couldn't help but follow you around. We hadn't met yet and I needed to be close." He hadn't fully understood it then, but he now knew he had done it because he literally couldn't stay away.

Ted appeared around the corner, obviously worried about his friend, and the earlier jealousy rose in Shahin's throat again. Why was Cai choosing to hang out with another man? He bit his tongue, certain that if he opened his mouth, he was going to say something he'd regret later.

Cai glanced at Ted and then back at Shahin. "I don't have time for this. Your story sounds ridiculous—the whole thing is ridiculous. I was going to say we're through, but we were never a couple. So let's just end this before it really starts. Less painful for both of us."

Fire collected behind Shahin's eyes, the tears burning their way out but never quite making it. He watched as Cai turned and left with Ted in tow. His heart couldn't decide whether to be angry or sad. Could you be both at the same time?

After standing there for a few moments, staring at the walls, Shahin left the coffeehouse, got on his bike, and rode at high speed. This wasn't him. He was not the kind of man to pine over a lost lover. They usually did the pining. He always rolled on, oblivious to pain and heartache. *I have to snap out of it.* Determined to forget Cai and his own feelings, Shahin rode to a local bar. He was going to drown his sorrows in booze and sex.

It didn't take him long to find out it wasn't that simple. Shortly after sitting on one of the high stools in the bar and ordering a scotch on ice, he could no longer ignore the pull. It was a strange sensation that started deep in his gut, traveled to his every extremity until his whole body was burning and hurting from yearning. Desire for one man. No one else would do. There would be no relief for him. Not tonight, not ever.

CHAPTER EIGHT

SOUL MATES

"**W**here the hell are you?" Lyra didn't sound too happy. He couldn't blame her. He was almost an hour late for their dinner. "Zack is seriously annoyed. You know how cranky he gets when he's hungry." Cai doubted very much that placid, gentle Zack was the one who was annoyed.

"I'm on my way," he lied. He was nowhere near the restaurant. Or his house. "I'll be there in a wink. Tell Zack to go ahead and start eating without me."

"We haven't even ordered. The waiters are starting to give us some dirty looks." He could imagine his sister making faces at the poor unsuspecting waiters as they passed her table.

"Just order for me. You know what I like." Cai was itching to get off the phone, uncomfortable as he was about lying to Lyra and of what he was really doing.

"I'll order the most expensive things on the menu and put it on your tab." *Petulant as usual.* "It serves you right for not being here on time." Cai chuckled gently and hung up.

Through the windshield he could see the house across the road, illuminated like a Christmas tree. Shahin had not been lying when he told him his mother's house was huge. This was a mansion with two floors, a four-car garage, and windows to rival Buckingham Palace. A stream of people went in and out of the house, some lingering on the porch, their breaths visible in the cold night air. He could understand now why Shahin had chosen to live on his own. It was a madhouse. What kind of family lived like that, almost twenty people to one house? He had heard of the Roma, who from their traditional nomadic lives had settled into large clan-like estates where the whole family lived together. But the Halcóns were not Roma, despite their European origin. Maybe it had something to do with the fact they were shifters. Cai was still having trouble wrapping his head around the idea. Sometimes he thought he'd imagined that whole conversation, or dreamed it perhaps. It was truly insane to think that anyone could morph from a human body to that of an animal.

He closed his eyes and imagined beautiful Shahin changing from his human form into that of a hawk. His tattooed arms shifting from flesh and bone to feathery wings, his stunning lips elongating into the majestic beak, his feet stretching and thinning out into talons.

Cai felt a tightening in his gut. He had always thought hawks to be majestic birds, graceful and strong, fierce and wild. Like Shahin.

Had Shahin been telling the truth about being his soul mate? About the pull? Cai hadn't slept well since he had left. In fact, he hadn't felt very well either. Symptoms of what he thought was a bad cold coming on had made him miserable ever since. Headaches, achy muscles, loss of appetite—and a dull pain in the middle of his chest. He thought it may be a recurrence of his old ulcer, or just plain acid reflux because of stress, but he had also lost his ability to focus exclusively on his work when at the office. His painting was the only thing that seemed to soothe him lately, but even that was beginning to lose its power. What was wrong with him?

I'm losing my mind. If these feelings wrenching him apart were not proof enough, this most definitely was— sitting in his car across from the Halcón's family home, watching. Watching what? Had he hoped Shahin would be there and that he would catch a glimpse of the tall, handsome man? *Shit. I'm turning into a stalker.* He chuckled to himself. What kind of person was he to be mad at Shahin for something he was now doing himself?

He turned the key in the ignition and drove away, an uncomfortable nagging feeling in his chest. *Did I judge him too quickly?* Had he been somehow looking for an excuse to break it off with Shahin before it got too serious? Was it possible that he was so scared of another heartbreak that he was willing to ruin this relationship even before it started?

I was a jerk to Shahin, and for what reason exactly? What had he accomplished? He had managed to turn himself into a stalker, skulking away under cover of the night, not sure of what he was looking for.

To be near him. The answer came to him suddenly. He was looking for ways to be near Shahin. Did this mean Shahin was right? That this thing he called "the pull" was real, and what he felt was the physical and emotional need to be close to his soul mate?

Resolved not to dwell on these rather unsettling ideas, Cai drove faster than he normally would downtown where he was to meet his sister and her boyfriend for dinner. They were already eating by the time he walked through the front door. Lyra gave him one of her famous icy looks, the kind that could freeze magma, as he sat down at the table.

"Sorry, guys. I was detained at work." Lies never sat well with him and even though it wasn't anything major, he felt the sting of the deceit in his throat.

"Bullshit, Cai. I called Ted and he said you had left work a long time ago." Caught, like he'd known he would be. He coughed and focused on the *zuppa di pesce* in front of him. The steaming, delicious-looking fish stew was a much friendlier sight than his sister's scowling face. "You look like hell, brother."

Zack jumped to his rescue. "Will you give the man a break? So he's a little late, no big deal."

Were the fire in her eyes real, he would have been a charred piece of meat.

Lyra turned her eyes back to her brother. "You look like shit. Are you sick or something?" Cai looked up, a bit surprised by the comment. True, he had not been feeling good for the last few days and several people at work had asked him the same question, but Lyra never seemed to notice that kind of thing. Did he really look that bad? "You look like you've lost weight."

Cai shivered, reminded of what Shahin had said about the deep connection between soul mates and how not being close to each other caused them pain. Was that what was happening to him? Was he getting sick because of the distance he had put between them?

"I'm fine. Just a little under the weather." He scooped a spoonful of the stew and brought it up to his mouth. It was deliciously warm, soothing his chilled body from the inside out. Why was he so cold? He rarely felt cold even during the dead of winter, so why was he shivering? "I may be getting a cold."

Lyra studied him, her chin resting on her hands. The plate in front of her was practically empty, which meant she had all the time in the world to focus on him. *Shit.* "Have you talked to your hot man?"

Cai choked on the *zuppa*. "He's not my man."

"Whatever. Anyone who watched you two gushing at each other knows differently." She turned to Zack. "You've seen Cai's starry eyes when he talks about Shahin. What do you think? Aren't they into each other big-time?"

As irritated as he was by his sister's usual lack of respect for his privacy, Cai felt sorry for Zack, who seemed utterly shocked for having been put on the spot. "I don't know—none of our business. Shouldn't we leave that for Cai and Shahin to decide?"

Lyra made a face at her boyfriend and turned back to Cai. "Come on, Cai. What exactly are you afraid of? You're obviously into him and, man, is he into you! You look worse than you did when you broke up with Jack."

He took a deep breath before speaking. "Lyra, my favorite and only sister, please let me take care of my love life myself, will you? There are things about this whole thing that you don't know. I have a lot to think through and you're not helping with your constant meddling."

Lyra pretended to pout, her lip sticking out like a sulky child's. "I love you and worry about you, Cai. You deserve someone awesome in your life. Someone who will love you and keep you warm at night. Don't let your fear get in the way."

"How's the stew?" Zack's question was so unexpected and out of place, they both stared at him for a moment before bursting out laughing. "What? What did I say?"

They were the last ones to leave the restaurant that night. After they said their farewells, Cai got in his car and began the short drive home. Shivers were still running through his body and a dull headache throbbed behind his eyes. What if it was true? That distance between them made them physically sick? Was Shahin feeling the same way? There was only one way to find out.

Making a U-turn at the next intersection, Cai headed toward Shahin's house on the outskirts of town. It was time for him to stop being scared of what might happen and face facts head-on. He was going to find out the truth—or lack thereof—of the hawk-man's claims.

Cai now understood why Shahin had chosen to live in such an isolated place. It gave him the perfect protection from prying eyes every time he morphed into his animal. Not for the first time, Cai's body responded to the idea of Shahin as a hawk, a magnificent bird of prey. He parked the car by the side of the house and sat for a few minutes, his hand playing with the key Shahin had left him that ill-fated morning.

Making a decision, Cai exited the car and walked to the front of the house. He was still shivering and his hand shook, making it difficult to insert the key in the hole. After a few attempts, he finally managed to unlock and open the door. Even though Shahin had given him the key it still felt strange and wrong to be entering his house without his knowledge. *Who is the stalker now?*

Cai had never been to Shahin's house, but somehow his body knew exactly which way to go. Whatever connected them pulled him up the stairs and into the first room on the right. The shivering had subsided, and anticipation had taken its place. Shahin had been telling the truth. Now that he was there, standing outside his room, the pain was gone, but the yearning was back full force.

At that moment, there was no doubt in his mind—Shahin was indeed his mate for life. Cai took a deep breath and opened the door.

THE KEEN EARS OF THE hawk heard it before his human counterpart did—footsteps coming up the stairs—and his heart recognized Cai before he laid eyes on him. His soul mate was coming.

Shahin wanted to jump out of bed and run to him, wrap himself around Cai's body and kiss him until they were both out of breath. But he waited instead. This decision had to come from Cai. Let him make the first move. He forced himself to lie back and stay still, listening. He heard Cai's breathing, fast and shallow, his steps slow and hesitant. He strained his ears and heard the beat of his mate's heart, a symphony to his senses. Shahin closed his eyes and took a long, calming breath. It was so strange to feel both excited and scared of what Cai would say or do once he opened that door.

Would he open the door?

The footsteps stopped and all he could hear for a few moments was the rapid rhythm of both Cai's and his hearts, beating in unison even while still separated. Desire burned in the pit of his stomach, a bittersweet feeling that made him quiver. *Come in, Cai. Please come in.*

His own breath had become fast and erratic as a weight settled on his chest.

The steps resumed, and he heard the telling click of the door handle being pushed down. He held his breath, afraid he would yell out in feverish anticipation. The door creaked open, a ray of light from the hallway slipping in through the gap and framing Cai's tall body in a halo. Like an angel's.

Cai closed the door behind him, the glow from the night-light blurring the edges of reality as he quietly approached the bed. Shahin held on to the edge of the bed, stopping himself from pouncing on the man he loved. *Patience, idiot, patience.* Cai was not impulsive or thoughtless like he was. He must respect Cai's sensibilities, be aware of his needs. And Cai needed to do this in his own time.

Shahin watched, fascinated, as Cai removed his coat, then his shoes and shirt. His heart was beating even faster now, his whole body tingling. Cai finished undressing and Shahin cursed the dimness of the room. He wanted to see his mate's body, bare and vulnerable, but he could only guess at what it looked like. Cai reached the edge of the bed and slid between the sheets beside Shahin. His naked body touched Cai's and he couldn't control it anymore. He flopped to his side and wrapped his hands around Cai, pulling him closer to him.

"What took you so long?" His voice was hoarse from desire, his body stretching along Cai's, relishing the warmth of the other man.

Cai buried his face in the crook of his neck and kissed him. "I'm sorry, Shahin." The warmth of his lips sent millions of tiny electric shocks throughout Shahin's body. "I believe you."

Shahin pulled back to look into Cai's eyes. "What do you mean? Believe in what?"

The silver-haired man smiled and crushed his lips against Shahin's. "I believe in your soul mate theory," he whispered over his lips, caressing his mate beneath the sheets.

"Not a theory. A fact." As intoxicated as he was with the other man's touch, Shahin needed to make this point. "Didn't you feel it? The pain, the emptiness, the pull?"

Cai's hands had traveled to Shahin's hips and slid over to cup his buttocks. Shahin moaned. "Yes, I did. I was physically sick, but as I got closer to you the symptoms lessened." He pressed Shahin against him. "God, you feel good."

Unable to control himself any longer, Shahin flipped Cai under him and lowered his mouth to his, nibbling on his lower lip, delighting in his taste. "I've been dreaming of this since I first saw you." Trailing kisses down to Cai's chin, then over his neck, Shahin lingered on Cai's hard chest before continuing down. Cai's skin tasted of promises Shahin so wanted fulfilled. He looked up for a second and met Cai's hazel eyes. Even in the dim light, Shahin saw the stars in them. *I love this man.*

Cai was as hard as he was, swollen by the intensity of the inexplicable pull of the soul mates. Shahin lowered his mouth and tasted him, a frisson of pleasure going through him when Cai moaned and arched his hips against him, begging for more. Cai's hands landed on his head, pressing him closer as he rocked in sync with Shahin's stroking.

"I'm going to lose it, Shahin." He wanted Cai to lose all control, to allow his body to drown in a wave of sensory pleasure, and he wanted to be the one causing that wave. He wanted his mate to leave his armor behind and be his, body and soul.

ON THE VERGE OF CLIMAXING, Cai pressed himself harder against Shahin. It had been a long time since he had sex, but this was so much more than sex. Between Shahin and him there was a strange and strong connection that defied explanation. It was as if a sensory rope tied them together. What one felt, the other one did too. It amplified the sensation, it amplified the pleasure. It was exhilarating, as if spiraling through space and time; everything else around them was erased and rendered meaningless. Shahin and their connection were all that mattered at that moment.

"I want to feel you inside me." The demand surprised even him. Cai was not used to being the one calling the shots in a relationship. He had always been willing to go along with whatever his partner wanted, no demands on his part, no voicing any desires. Maybe he had never wanted anything this badly. Maybe his relationships up to this point had not been strong enough or exciting enough for him to *want*.

Shahin looked up, his blue eyes shining in the dark, and at that moment Cai would have sworn he saw the hawk—a blue-eyed hawk with a beautiful brown-gray feather-covered head and a white-speckled chest. The vision lasted only a few seconds but took his breath away. The man left behind was just as breathtaking as he made his way up Cai's body, seeking a kiss he was more than willing to yield to.

When their mouths parted, they were both winded. Cai could hear Shahin's heart beating a frenzied tune against his chest and his own heart. "Do you love me?" A loaded question for Cai, who was still getting used to the idea that this man he had known for a short time was his soul mate. His heart told him yes, but his ever-rational mind told him to be cautious, to hold off on declaring his love until later.

Unwilling to answer, Cai took charge again, rolling both of them around so that he was on top now. Their bodies were glued together, hard muscle against hard muscle. "Well? Are you going to do it or not?" Cai punctuated his question by sliding his hand low between them and caressing him.

Shahin moaned, touching his forehead to Cai's chest and arching up toward his mate's hand. "Yes. God, yes."

"Do you have a condom? Lube?"

Shahin stretched over and opened his nightstand drawer. Seconds later he waved the foil-wrapped prophylactic, ripped it open, and handed it to Cai. Straddling Shahin on his knees, Cai rolled the lubricated condom over his mate's arousal, delighting in the trembling and soft groan he incited.

"Take me." Who was this man? Cai hardly recognized himself, but he liked it.

Shahin, flipping him over and positioning himself behind Cai, brought his hand around his mate's hips and caressed him. "I love you, Cai. You may not love me yet, but a hawk is patient and persistent." He lowered his lips to Cai's shoulder blade and kissed him, running his tongue over his warm skin as he slid a lubricant-covered finger inside his mate. Cai gasped, but then relaxed against his probing. "Hawks make awesome lovers."

Cai laughed and rubbed his bottom against the hardness of Shahin's lower body and shivered in anticipation. "Will you stop talking and get on with it already?"

His mate didn't disappoint. Shahin eased his length inside him, and Cai yelled out in a mix of pleasure and pain, pressing back, wanting to be even closer to his mate. He was not going to last long. They danced together, their bodies bumping into each other, Shahin's hands stroking him from pain into ecstasy. There was a gathering of stars in the room about to explode into supernovas. Shahin grunted behind him and Cai felt his muscles contract and relax in spasms of pleasure just as he reached the edge and free-fell, the stars now inside him.

They both collapsed side by side on the bed, still connected, unwilling to pull apart. Shahin's arms cocooned Cai as he nuzzled and kissed his neck. Breathing returning to normal, Cai wondered briefly at the wonderful feeling of being finally home before he fell asleep.

IF SHAHIN HAD BEEN THE poetic kind, he would have thought Cai looked like an angel as he slept next to him. The wrinkles around his eyes, caused by whatever turmoil twirled in his mind, had been smoothed away by sleep. Shahin brushed a hand over his face, touching every hill and every valley, delighting in the coarse hair of his day-old stubble. Not satisfied, he explored further—his fingers sliding over and between the strands of short and soft silvery hair.

Damn, I'm hard again.

He leaned back into the pillow, his hand draped across Cai's chest. This was madness. Total and utter madness. How was it possible to be this connected to a non-shifter, a non-*cambiador*? It was unheard of and his flock was not going to like it. If his mother had already flipped over a simple crush, he could only imagine what she was going to do once she found out they had consummated their relationship. Yes, Cai had yet to profess his love back, but Shahin was certain it would happen. At least, he hoped it would happen. Wouldn't it be a hoot if he, who had always been the one breaking hearts, got his heart crushed by a full-human? He laughed softly.

"What are you laughing about, hawk-man?" Cai lay on his back, his hazel eyes trained on Shahin. A little smile danced on the corner of his lips. "You're not laughing at my awkward, old-man's body, are you?"

Shahin sat up, outraged. "What are you talking about, Cai?" Gripping the edges of the sheet covering both of them, he pulled it aside, uncovering Cai's naked body. He surveyed Cai with hungry eyes, one inch at a time. "All I see is gorgeousness." His husky voice betrayed the desire in his gut. "I love everything I see... and touch." He brushed a hand over Cai's chest and down to his abs. *Fuck. Not now.* "Stop being so fucking sexy, will you? We have to talk."

Cai laughed and pulled Shahin's arms until he fell on him. "We'll talk as soon as I taste you."

No talking happened for the rest of the morning. Finally, deliriously exhausted and sated, they lay together, legs still entwined, shoulders touching. Shahin found that he liked this new type of intimacy—the kind where he didn't run out the door as soon as sex was over, the kind where part of the fun was to linger in bed, talking in whispers and laughing at each other's jokes.

"How does it feel?" Shahin lifted an eyebrow at Cai's question. "Becoming a hawk. How is that even possible?"

Turning slightly, Shahin kissed Cai's cheek. "Don't ask me about the mechanics of it. I have no idea. It goes back so far in history, the true origins of our species kind of got lost in time. Some say it was a curse put on our family centuries ago. Others claim it is the result of some mutant genes created by radiation. Sort of like Spiderman." He snorted. "Who knows. But it goes back many generations."

"Will you one day become the hawk and not change back?" There was a note of fear in Cai's voice as he turned slightly to hide his face in the crook of Shahin's neck.

Shahin brushed his fingers across his mate's cheek and chuckled softly. "No, I will always change back to my human shape. It's not a permanent thing."

Cai leaned his face against Shahin's hand. "Who is in control when you're a hawk? You or the animal side of you?" Shahin smiled at him. "I have a lot of questions."

"It's okay to ask," Shahin assured him. "I'm always in charge, really. The only thing that changes radically is my body. If the hawk had control, I probably wouldn't have ended up in the hospital. My very human stupidity caused my downfall that night."

"Are you ever going to tell me what happened that night?" Cai leaned on a bent arm. "And while we're talking about that, how did you heal so fast? Your wound is totally healed." Cai's fingers tracing the length of his scar made him shiver and sigh.

"I shouldn't have been flying at night, but I had been dying to do it all day long." Shahin played with the sparse coat of hair on

Cai's chest and was pleased to see his mate respond. "I was attacked by a great horned owl on my way home. It nearly killed me, but I managed to morph into my human form right before it dropped me. I was close to your house so I crawled there."

Cai draped his leg over Shahin's and swept his hand along his neck, caressing his tattoo all the way down to his bicep where it stopped. "I love your tattoo," he whispered, eyes following the path of his fingers. "Why roses?"

Quivering in pleasure, Shahin took his mate's lower lip between his teeth and gently nibbled and pulled. Cai's reaction against his thigh triggered a smile. "Immortal love. Even though I really didn't believe in the stories, I liked the idea of a love so strong it would defy death itself."

Cai flickered his tongue against his lips, lingering over his snake bite. "Who would have thought? The rebel has a romantic side." Shahin caught his tongue with his lips and swallowed him whole. Would this hunger for his soul mate ever fade?

CHAPTER NINE

TACOS & APPLE PIE

"You got laid!" Lyra's explosive voice caught Cai by surprise and he dropped the knife. "Oh my God, you finally got laid."

Cai picked up the knife from the floor and ran it under the water in the sink. "You act like I was a virgin or something." He chopped a few more carrots, trying to be mad at his sister's unwarranted reaction but smiling instead. His heart was doing a happy jig in his chest, and try as he might, he couldn't wipe out the idiotic smile he'd been wearing since the night Shahin had first made love to him.

"You might as well be one. You hadn't seen any action since your ass of a boyfriend left." Not totally true. He'd had a couple meaningless trysts, but he wasn't going to contradict her. Being the baby sister never stopped Lyra from acting as if she was his mom. It was often as annoying as it was endearing.

Lyra leaned against a kitchen cabinet, munching on the carrots he was diligently chopping for snacks. She looked as if she had just come in from walking through a wind tunnel, her hair in total disarray. Zack was out of town again, and she'd stayed over—and had yet to bother showering.

"Not to ruin your fun or anything. I know how much you enjoy snooping into my love life, but you are a little ripe, sister." He popped a couple slices in his mouth and crunched down.

Looking baffled, his sister bit another piece of carrot, nibbling it around the edges like a rabbit. "I have no idea what you're talking about. I took a shower two days ago. Like Mom always said, water is good for the fish."

Cai threw his head back and chuckled. "Mom never said any such thing. She was always on our case about personal hygiene." The simple thought of his mother brought the familiar sting of tears to the back of his eyes. "She did often mention though how she wished her only daughter was more ladylike."

Picking up another piece of carrot, she threw it at Cai. "Liar." She peeled herself off the counter and moved across the kitchen and into the living room. "You're not in the safe zone yet, bro. I will come back to totally badger you about your new hot boyfriend."

With a shake of his head and a soft chuckle, Cai wiped his hands on a kitchen towel and went up to his room to change. They were meeting Shahin for an early dinner at a local restaurant and he was as giddy as a teenage boy on his first date. After a thorough search of his closet, he decided he needed to shop for new clothes, surprised and dismayed that his wardrobe looked old and out of fashion. Feeling stupid for his adolescent attitude, he settled for a pair of jeans and a soft white sweater.

"You look gorgeous, Cinderella." His sister was standing in the doorway, her arms crossed over her chest and a smirk on her lips. "Shahin will have trouble keeping his undies on."

"Crass as usual, my socially inept sister." He picked a cashmere scarf from a drawer in his dresser and wrapped it around his neck.

Lyra approached and took over, pushing his hands away from the scarf. "Let me do it, Cai. It looks like you're wrapping a noose around your neck instead of a beautiful and—crap, this is cashmere. When did you buy this beauty? And how much did it set you back?"

"Man, you're like a puppy—easily distracted." Cai sat on the edge of his bed and suffered through his sister's ministrations as she tied the scarf, unwrapped it, and tied it again. "You will behave, right? Shahin is important to me." He hoped he wouldn't regret the admission.

Lyra puckered her lips in a poor imitation of a pout. "Of course I will, Cai. Who do you take me for?" Once more, she removed the cashmere item from around his neck and tied it in a different way.

"A spoiled brat who doesn't know when to shut up." He laughed, letting her know he was only teasing her. "But seriously,

Shahin is—special."

Without warning, Lyra threw her arms around his neck and drew him to her in a hug. "I'm so happy you've found someone worthy of you, Cai. You deserve the stars, and so far, you got nothing but worms."

Cai enjoyed his sister's hug for a moment, memories of when they were children flooding his mind. How she used to run like a maniac, her dark pigtails bouncing around her pixie face, and throw herself into his arms after school. There were six years between them and even though he had often despaired over his overenthusiastic sister, she had always brought on his knight-in-shining-armor side. Not that she needed protection. She was perfectly—and had always been—capable of defending herself. In fact, she had been famous in high school for her left hook. Many teenage boys had rued the day they'd decided to mess with her. He laughed under his breath.

"What are you laughing at?" Lyra unlatched herself from her brother and frowned. "You look like the Cheshire cat after swallowing a bird—or a rat."

"I was thinking of how you used to pester me constantly when you were little." He laughed again, adjusting the scarf around his neck. "I guess not much has changed since then."

Lyra punched his upper arm. "Except I now could take you easily. Weakling." She turned her back and walked out of the room. "You better hurry up putting on your makeup, Cinderella, or Shahin will be having dinner alone."

It was just getting dark when they arrived at Zandra's Taqueria. As soon as they entered, Cai scanned the room and found him; Shahin was sitting alone at a corner table, immersed in thought. Inside Cai, a small storm began to brew. From the depths of his gut, the whirlwinds spun and shook everything in their path, blowing his heart up in his throat where it beat so fiercely he thought he'd choke. There it was again. The pull, that inexplicable force that drew the two together with such power they were helpless against it.

"There he is," said Lyra, holding on to Cai's hand and pulling in that direction. As if he needed prodding. "Hey, Shahin, your boyfriend is here."

Cai pulled on her hand. "You have no couth whatsoever, Lyra." People turned to stare at them as they navigated the maze of tables and chairs between them and the hawk-man. "Nice. We just became the main attraction tonight." Thankfully there weren't that many people in the small Mexican restaurant, so the damage done by his crazy sister was minimal.

Shahin lifted the oceans he had for eyes and met Cai's gaze. His heart dropped a few inches, leaving him gasping for breath. Every time he gazed into his mate's eyes he saw infinity. Shahin stood up as they approached, pulling a chair for Lyra who hummed in appreciation. Then he took a few steps around the table, grabbed Cai by the peacoat's lapels, and crushed his lips against his. The heat created between them spread from his lips to his neck and then the rest of his body and took control. For a moment he forgot where they were and nudged Shahin's lips open with his tongue, desperate to taste his mate again.

A little cough brought him back to here and now. "Shoving your tongue down his throat in the middle of a restaurant is probably not the best way to not attract attention." Lyra was staring up at them, a smile on her lips and a twinkle in her eyes. "Can we eat or are you guys going to just make out through dinner?"

Cai's face burned as he furtively glanced around him. A few patrons were watching the two of them as they pulled apart and sat at the table.

Shahin laughed. Nothing seemed to faze him ever. "Well, they got a taste of what will go on behind the curtains later tonight." Cai's blush deepened. "You're so fucking cute when you blush."

A server came over with several menus, bowls of chips and salsa, and glasses of water. Lyra, always the hungry one, salivated over the menu while crunching away at the chips as if she hadn't eaten in days.

"I love their bison tacos," she said with the enthusiasm of an art lover faced with a DaVinci. "Let's get a double order."

Amused, Shahin laughed. "For someone as skinny as you are you sure eat a lot." She gave him a brief look and returned to her analysis of the menu. Shahin looked at Cai, reaching out for his hand over the table. "Let me guess. You want the grilled shrimp tacos, right?"

Cai was touched that in the short time they had known each other, his mate already seemed to know him better than the man with whom he had shared so many years of his life. He nodded. "You? Meat, I'm sure."

With a squeeze of his hand, Shahin shrugged. "I don't usually eat in Mexican restaurants because their food is too cooked for my taste." Throwing a sly glance at Lyra, he whispered, "The hawk likes food a little more on the raw side."

"Hawk?" Lyra had always had crazy good hearing. "What hawk?"

Cai thought he should come to the rescue. Eventually he wanted to share that bit of surprising and unbelievable information about his soul mate with his sister, but for now he wanted to keep the drama to a minimum. "It's a private joke."

Lyra dropped the menu and smiled, batting her eyes like a Southern belle in an old black-and-white movie. "Aww, you already have private jokes. That's so adorable."

"Nobody ever called me adorable, but I forgive you because you're my soul mate's sister." Shahin squeezed his hand again, and Cai squirmed in his seat, his jeans suddenly becoming uncomfortably tight.

"Oh, my God. You're killing me, Shahin," Lyra exclaimed. "Soul mate? How sweet is that?"

Trying to find a distraction—anything—from the conversation, Cai waved the server over and placed the order, his mate finally deciding on the chicken tacos.

The food came out quickly and piping hot, the spicy scents wafting up from the plate to their noses, tantalizing and comforting all at once. They ate and talked companionably for a while as the restaurant began to fill with a larger crowd.

"How come we had to eat so early?" Lyra asked. "Not that I mind. I was famished."

"I'm expected at my family's house for our weekly gathering." Shahin stole a glance at Cai, reminding him of his mother's visit that night a few weeks ago. "I already pissed off my mom enough by living away from them. If I don't show up at these dinners, I'd never hear the end of it."

"At least you still have a mom." The sadness in her voice gripped him by the throat. Cai reached out to take her hand in his. "Where's your dad?"

"God only knows." Shahin's nose was white, covered in cinnamon sugar from the *zeppole* he was eating. Cai grabbed a napkin and wiped it clean, delighting in the familiarity of the gesture. Shahin smiled at him, a smile that could melt the iciest of hearts. "He's a big mystery in our family, and no one is allowed to mention him. He's the unwanted man, the pariah." He laughed. "What my mom says goes. She's been the Big Boss for a long time, being the oldest. Being the flock's matron, no one is willing to question her. Ever and about anything."

Lyra wiped her mouth with a napkin and bent over the table to come closer to the two men. "Aren't you curious?"

Cai took his last bite of the *zeppole*, an Italian-type donut that was hard to eat without making a mess of yourself. Shahin stood up, bent over the table toward him, and licked the sugar from Cai's lips. *My jeans are going to explode.* The wicked hawk-man winked at him as he sat back down. Cai didn't dare look at his sister, so he lowered his eyes to the table.

"A little curious, but not enough to go looking for him, I guess." Shahin had sneaked a hand under the table to lay it on Cai's upper thigh. "I mean, if he had interest in us, he would have come looking for us a long time ago, right? I'm the middle child, but even my oldest sibling doesn't remember him at all."

Cai gulped. The restaurant was suddenly very hot, and he was in need of a very cold shower. There was no way he was getting up and walking out anytime soon. Shahin, on the other hand, stood up, blissfully indifferent to his obvious state of arousal, and prepared to leave.

"I'll pay for dinner on my way out. Great dinner, even better company. Thank you, guys." He took a step closer to Cai and kissed him, hard and long. "I will stop by later." A whisper pregnant with promise.

Cai watched him slipping into his leather jacket on his way to the door. He couldn't get his eyes off his man as he stopped by the register to pay for dinner, turned around briefly to wave goodbye, and vanished through the front door into the dark street like a vision. Cai held his breath, afraid he had imagined his soul mate. Afraid that he would wake up and find out it had all been a beautiful dream.

IF SOMEONE STUCK A HAND down his throat, grabbed his innards, and pulled them from the inside out, it would still be less painful than these evenings around his mother. As the loyal son he was, Shahin faithfully attended these weekly gatherings at his matriarch's house—out of guilt mostly, but still. The only thing that brightened these agonizing events was his sister's amazing apple pie. He could never get enough. In fact, he was willing to fight with his young nieces and nephews for the last slice.

Mom was particularly cantankerous that night, never giving up on the chance to jab at everything he said. Shahin was surprised she had yet to make a snide comment about his new boyfriend. As he sat at the table, surrounded by his loud flock, he wondered about his father. He hadn't thought about him in a long time, but the conversation he'd had with Cai and Lyra earlier had renewed his long-forgotten curiosity about the mysterious man who had fathered the Halcóns. His mother very rarely mentioned him unless she absolutely had to, and even then, she always referred to him as the "asshole" or the "jackass." Whatever the man had done, she obviously was not about to forgive him in this lifetime.

"Have you heard?" His mother's voice brought all the conversations to a halt, and every eye turned her way. "Your witless brother is dating a non-*cambiador.*" There was a general intake of air from around the table. "Yes, he doesn't believe in the curse and is willing to risk his life for this full-human."

Maya turned around, her mouth half-open and an expression of utter horror in her eyes. "What are you doing, Shahin? You know how dangerous that is."

"That's an old wives' tale." Now that he knew the old myth of the soul mate was an actual fact, he was no longer 100 percent sure the stories about the risks of mating with a full-human were a total fabrication. He hid his hesitation with a giant forkful of pie, washed down with a gulp of his mom's coffee. "This pie is amazing, Maya."

"Mom helped me bake it." That was a first. Mom left all the baking to her daughter and a couple of her sisters. Her specialty was sharp barbs and spiteful comebacks. Not for the first time, Shahin wondered if she had always been like that or if some event in her life had turned her bitter and cranky. "But don't try to distract me. Are you freaking crazy? Mating with a full-human can kill you."

"Well, it's too late to go back now. Done deal." The part of him that always rebelled against anything and everything rejoiced in the shocking looks his comment provoked. "We fucked and I'm still alive."

Sal's wife, Maria, tried to cover her oldest child's ears. "Will you watch your mouth, Shahin? There are children in the room."

Shahin was livid. When had he become the night's entertainment? Why was everyone so interested in his love life?

"You know very well that it is not the physical act—as you so colorfully put it—that is the problem," his sister said. "It's when you bond emotionally. Please tell me you are only having a casual affair with this man."

Shahin drank another big gulp of coffee so he could not snap back at his sister, possibly the only family member he truly liked. But the words were burning on his tongue.

"Your brother wouldn't be that misguided." It was another sarcasm-laden comment from his mother.

He'd had it. He jumped to his feet, almost taking the tablecloth along with him, and slammed his fist on the table. "I love Cai. Love him, do you understand? He's my soul mate and no stupid old myth is going to keep me away from him."

Several of the younger Halcóns began crying, startled by his outburst. Shahin walked away.

"Son, you think you're immune to the old ways, but you're not." His mother had followed him into the hallway. "I don't want you to get hurt. You'll get sick and could very well die. *Cambiadores* and full-humans are not compatible. You must let him go. Now."

Shahin turned around so fast, dizziness overtook him for a moment. "Stop trying to control my life, Mom. You're a miserable woman who can't stand to see anyone happy around her. Not even your kids. I'm sick of it."

He slammed the door behind him, guilt gnawing at his heels but too upset to care. He needed to see Cai, to feel his heart beating against him, to share his warmth with the man he loved. Shahin climbed on his motorcycle and sped away without a helmet. Damn caution, damn everything else. Only one thing mattered. One person. One man.

He couldn't be sure of how long it took him to get to Cai's house. The lights were on even though it was past midnight. The Halcóns went to bed late and woke up early. The perks of being half hawk. Cai was waiting up for him. His heart shifted a little, the topography of his being changing ever so slightly. He walked to the door and knocked, the blood running through his veins at such speed he thought he could actually hear it.

The lock clicked, and Cai was standing in front of him. He was perfect, from his silver hair to the light stubble on his face. Dressed in a simple pair of gray joggers and a white Henley, Cai couldn't be more handsome. *God, when did I become so cheesy?* Since meeting Cai, Shahin couldn't remember how his life had been before him. Must not have been that exciting, because the only thing he could remember was the time he'd spent with Cai.

"Come in." Cai didn't need to invite him twice. Shahin stepped in the hallway, locked his hands around Cai's waist, and kissed him. Entwined, they stumbled around until Cai's back met the wall. Shahin pressed himself against him, hungrily exploring Cai's mouth with his tongue. He couldn't get enough of his taste, his scent, his everything.

"I love you," he whispered into Cai's mouth. "Nothing is going to make me give you up. Not even the witch I call my mom."

Cai chuckled against his lips, pausing to run a tongue over his snake bite. "Did you drink?"

Funny he would ask that. For once, Shahin had not drunk anything other than soda, but he did feel slightly intoxicated—blurred vision and lightly nauseated. Too much pie? Or was he just drunk on the headiness that was Cai?

"I dinna drink a' all." Was he slurring his speech? The room began moving unexpectedly and he had to hold on to Cai not to fall. "Earthquake."

The corners of Cai's eyes crinkled. "Earthquake? What are you talking about, Shahin? Are you okay?"

"The room just moved." Shahin gagged as a wave of nausea ran through his body. "I think I'm going to be sick." Cai barely had time to step aside before Shahin's stomach contents came pouring out of his mouth and onto the wooden floors.

Cai held Shahin's head as he retched until there was nothing in his stomach besides bile. "This is becoming a very nasty habit." Cai helped him to the couch and handed him a wet kitchen towel to wipe his mouth with. "You getting sick in my house."

"Sorry, Cai. I was fine and then—" He gagged again. "Fuck, I feel like crap. What the hell?"

Laughing softly, Cai sat next to him and held his hand. "Probably something you ate."

Shahin shook his head and immediately wished he hadn't. The room swam in front of his eyes as another wave of nausea wreaked chaos in his stomach. "All I ate was my mother's food and my sister's pie. Same old, same old." Cai touched his forehead. "I'm a hawk. I eat raw meat. There isn't much that can make me sick."

"You don't have a temperature. Let me get you some ginger ale."

Before Cai could get up, Shahin grabbed his hand and held him in place. "Stay here with me, please. I feel like I'm going to pass out."

He held on to Cai's hand as if to a lifeline. *Please, don't let me go.* He was not afraid of much, but this was scaring him. He had never felt so sick. The room hadn't ceased to move and was buried under a cloud of blurry fumes, as if his eyes had stopped working properly. Arctic air had taken residence inside his body and assailed him with uncontrollable shivering. Cai stretched out to pick a throw from the bottom of the couch and spread it over Shahin. Afraid of losing touch with the tenuous thread holding him to consciousness, Shahin fought to keep his eyes open, but this was a battle he was not going to win. Darkness took over him.

When he opened his eyes later, Cai was not there. In a panic, he sprang to his feet and almost fell back down again, his head swimming from the sudden movement. "Ouch." A whole step team was performing an elaborate and loud routine inside his head. "Cai, where are you?"

His handsome mate appeared around the corner from the

kitchen, wiping his hands on a towel. "What's wrong? Are you okay?"

Shahin rubbed his temples, trying to massage the pain away. "I got a fucking headache." He tried to smile but was sure it came out more as a grimace. "Where were you? I thought you'd left." Did he sound desperate?

"I was cleaning up. You kind of made a huge mess on my floor." Cai chuckled and came to sit down next to him. "You seem to have a gift for surprising me." He touched Shahin's face and he leaned against his hand automatically, closing his eyes to better enjoy the sensory delight his touch always incited.

"I've never felt so bad in my life. Holy shit, what kind of bug did I catch?" He leaned against Cai's shoulder and inhaled his heady scent. "It must have been one of my nieces or nephews. They're cute little germ factories."

Cai slid his arm over his shoulders. "But you're feeling better now? Are you sure you don't want to go to the doctor?"

Lifting his head and still a little sore, Shahin rubbed his eyes. "Much better, even though it feels like I have a tractor running inside my head. Do you have some Tylenol somewhere?"

"In the bathroom," Cai said, piercing eyes studying him. "Maybe a bath is just what the doctor ordered. A little lavender to relax and for the headache." A hot bath sounded heavenly. He nodded. "I'll go run the water and get you some pills. Drink that water. You need to hydrate after all you spilled out."

Cai's guest bathroom had a large, deep garden tub, which was now filled halfway. The scent of lavender wafted from the hot water, inviting and tantalizing while he brushed his teeth. Cai had left him there and closed the door behind him, giving him a measure of privacy he didn't want. Shahin was almost fully recovered from his bout with whatever had hit him. He undressed and slipped into the tub, every muscle in his body relaxing as the hot water washed over him. He lay there for a few moments, eyes closed, head against the edge of the tub, but something was missing.

"Cai," he called suddenly, sitting up and splashing some of the water onto the floor. "Can you come here?"

His soul mate opened the door slowly, almost fearfully, and peeked through the opening. "Is something wrong? Are you feeling sick again?"

Shahin smiled. "Can you come closer?"

One step at a time, a shy smile growing on his lips, Cai approached the bathtub. "What do you need?" His eyes roamed Shahin's body from top to bottom, his Adam's apple bobbing up and down. The gray joggers Cai wore couldn't hide how he felt about his lover.

"I want you in here with me." He was shaking again, but this time not from the cold but from pure desire. "Please."

Cai gulped again, eyes glued to his. For a moment Shahin thought he wouldn't move, but Cai surprised him again by suddenly beginning to strip. One piece of clothing at a time, his pace maddeningly slow, deliberate and teasing. Shahin swelled in response as his mate climbed over the edge of the bathtub and slid along his body, skin against skin, hardness against hardness. The hawk-man stopped breathing for a second or two, delighted with the contact.

Their lips met briefly before Cai pulled apart and whispered over them, "Tell me, is throwing up over your lover's floor some kind of weird hawk mating ritual?"

Shahin burst out laughing. "No, but this is." In one smooth and unexpected move, he flipped Cai under him, more water spilling over the edges of the tub. "I'm going to love you so hard, you'll be begging for mercy." As soon as the words were out, he regretted them, afraid Cai would think him too aggressive.

But Cai surprised him yet again. "Bring it on, hawk-man. Bring it on."

CHAPTER TEN

FREE-FALLING

Blue. Why was the color blue associated with being sad? He loved blue more than any other in the color wheel. It calmed him, soothed his soul, and made him happy. Not sad. Not once. As he splashed another shade of blue over the canvas, Cai thought of his mother, the gentle artist with a heart of gold who had inspired him and his sister to follow their dreams. His father had always been the more pragmatic parent, counterbalancing his mom's penchant for esoteric and idealistic thought. As much as Cai admired his mom, it was rather ironic that he had followed his dad's advice and chosen a more down-to-earth career than the one he had always loved—that of an artist.

Taking a couple steps away from the easel, he studied his work with an analytical eye. It was good, great even, reflecting the sense of well-being and happiness he was trying to convey. The giddy feeling he carried around in his heart every hour of the day now. He was falling head over heels for the exciting and wild Shahin. God knew he had fought his own heart with all his might, refusing to fall in love. But it had all been futile. In the end, and even though he hadn't quite admitted it to his mate, he had taken the bait, hook, and sinker. He was totally and helplessly in love.

A streak of red amid all the blue made him cringe. The worry that had been gnawing at him lately. Shahin had been sick often for the past couple weeks—nauseated, dizzy, assailed by unexplained tremors. His usual healthy visage was quickly being replaced by pale skin and dark circles around his eyes. Stubbornly he refused to see a doctor, claiming he was probably just suffering from a stomach virus. But Cai could tell he was worried too. Whatever was going through his mind, Shahin kept to himself, a fact that worried Cai even more. Why wouldn't he share his thoughts with him?

Shahin's mysterious illness came and went for no perceivable reason. One minute, he would be practically comatose, his strength fully recovered the next. It was baffling and troublesome.

A knock on the door yanked him out of his thoughts. He cleaned his paint-stained hands on a towel and ran downstairs. There was no need to ask who it was. As he walked down the stairs, he felt it—the pull. Every time he thought it couldn't get any stronger, it did. Each time they were together, the invisible link between them strengthened and tightened.

Cai's breathing quickened at the sight of his soul mate. He couldn't help but admire the man's beauty—young, vibrant, with thick light brown hair and ocean blue eyes to make all others seem drab and ordinary. "You're beautiful." It was more of a sigh than a compliment. It was hard for him to believe even now that he could be connected in such an intimate and deep way to this exquisite wild creature.

He couldn't say anything else. Shahin covered Cai's mouth with his, his arms enveloping and pinning him between the wall and his body. They breathed each other in, bodies pressed so closely together it was hard to tell them apart. Cai felt his mate's desire grow against him and swelled in response. It was crazy how much he craved Shahin. All the time.

This time they didn't make it to the bed. Entwined in each other, they made love right there on the floor by the front door. Later, they sat together, sated and out of breath—Cai's bare back against the wall with Shahin settled between his legs, naked bodies still half-entangled.

Cai planted a kiss behind Shahin's ear. "Are you feeling better today?" His mate nodded, breathless from their lovemaking. "You really should go to a doctor."

Shahin twisted his neck around and sought his lips for another kiss. "I'll be fine. Hawks heal fast and don't get sick often."

"I hate to be the bearer of bad news, but you have been sick often lately and the healing doesn't seem to be going too well either." Cai flattened his hands on his mate's abs, awestruck by how firm and warm they were. Predictably he began feeling the stirrings of desire again. *Shit. What's wrong with me?* He had not been this sexual before. Normal, like any other guy, yes. But this almost constant hunger for this man was as puzzling as it was thrilling.

Shahin laughed. "You want to go again so soon?" Teasingly, his lover pressed himself harder against him. Cai gasped.

"It's all your fault, Sha," Cai said. Shahin turned around and knelt between Cai's outstretched legs, facing him. "You're so freaking hot. I can't keep my hands off you."

Bending forward, Shahin showered Cai with kisses from his face down to his chest where he lingered over the hard muscles, his hands sliding along the bare skin of his waist and dipping down to cup his buttocks. "I'm up for it if you are," Shahin whispered as he continued his trek downward to wrap his lips around Cai's growing arousal. Cai was lost to the pleasure of his lover's warm mouth expertly coaxing him into ecstasy.

Eventually, they found their way to bed, but Cai couldn't tell how. When he was with Shahin, he lost all sense of time and reality. His soul mate was all that mattered as the whole world faded into the background. He nuzzled against Shahin's neck, drunk on love.

"I love you." It was Shahin, half asleep already, hanging on to Cai as if afraid he'd vanish. "I don't want to ever lose you, love. Ever."

The tone of desperation in his voice made Cai pop his eyes wide open, suddenly very much awake. Why would he lose him? Even though Cai hadn't admitted to loving him yet, wasn't it obvious that he needed Shahin as much as he needed water or air?

"What do you mean by that?" But his mate was fast asleep. He was not as strong as he had been just a couple weeks ago. During one of their lovemaking sessions, Shahin had accidentally confessed to feeling so weak, he hadn't been able to change into a hawk in a while. Again, worry came to haunt him, and he lay in bed staring at his mate and wondering what he was hiding.

"WILL YOU STOP BEING SUCH a pain?" Shahin pulled on Cai's hand, urging him to move away from the motorcycle. "It's a surprise."

Groaning, Cai allowed his mate to forcibly guide him across the rocky terrain and closer to the edge of the precipice. "You're not going to throw me over the edge, are you?"

Shahin laughed. "No, even though you're making that possibility look very attractive right now." He had stopped by a group of bushes. "Wait here."

Disappearing for a few moments, Shahin went behind the bushes and uncovered his hiding place. He had made sure to store extra equipment for this occasion since he had been playing with the idea for a while now.

"I want you to know how it feels when I fly as a hawk," he said, dragging the bulky equipment from behind the bushes.

Cai's eyes widen. "What in heaven's name is that?"

"Wingsuit and parachutes." Shahin smiled at the expression of utter shock on his lover's face. "It's perfectly safe."

"For a hawk, maybe." Cai took a few steps backward and Shahin thought he was going to bolt. "Are you crazy? I can't do that."

Shahin's smile faded. "I really want to share this with you." *Before I'm gone.* He no longer thought that his emotional attachment to a full-human was harmless. He had been sick so many times, growing weaker every day, he couldn't deny reality any longer. His mother had been telling the truth about the dangers of an interspecies relationship. "I promise I'll keep you safe."

Cai smiled and drew him into a hug. "I will do this for you, but then I may have to kill you." They laughed together, holding each other in the cold mountain air.

Shahin showed Cai how to attach the parachute to his body and then slipped into his wingsuit. "You'll be diving on my back." Cai's mouth fell open. Shahin laughed. "Trust me."

"Have I ever told you how much I hate when people say that to me?" Nervously, he pulled on the buckles of the parachute. "And did I ever tell you I'm not too fond of heights either?"

Shahin wobbled toward the edge of the cliff. "Don't be a baby.

I'll be there all the way." Methodically he went over the safety details with his boyfriend. "In case of an emergency, you pull these. Got it?"

Cai seemed to have lost his ability to speak and nodded. He took a few steps closer and hugged Shahin. "These contraptions are not very love-friendly, are they?" They laughed. "Sha, I'm scared witless, but I really want to do this. For you. For us. I want to know how it feels, to be there with you in a way when you fly in your hawk wings."

They inched closer to kiss, but their helmets crashed together. "Again. Not a love-friendly getup."

Shahin chuckled and ambled closer to the edge, holding on to Cai's hands. "Get behind me and hold on to my neck. Once we jump, sit on my back and hold on to the straps on my shoulders." Shahin reached for the straps hanging along Cai's body and latched them to his suit. "When I give you the sign, deploy the parachute. Ready?"

The jump was different from his usual. With Cai's weight on top of him, he free-fell longer than usual, the vertiginous loss of control making his heart beat faster and his consciousness wavered for a moment. Cai was holding on to his neck for dear life as he opened his wings until the wind supported and lifted him slightly. They were going faster than he had ever gone before, and the icy air buffeted his face to numbness. Cai relaxed on his back. He smiled. So he was feeling it too—the amazing sensation of floating on air, of wafting up like perfume or smoke, wisps of flesh defying the laws of gravity, the laws of nature. It was exhilarating.

Together they made their way toward the ground at high speed, not unlike the other times he had done it. But today something was not right. Shahin felt dizzy, his sight blurring and wavering, arms feeling heavy and tired, reluctant to hold the wings open. Panic began rising up his throat—he couldn't pass out with Cai counting on him to land safely. But there was no mistaking the feeling. He was about to faint and kill both of them. Cursing under his breath, he fought the vertigo, the sense of fleeing consciousness, the weight on his head.

The ground was approaching fast, but he couldn't move his arms anymore to give Cai the signal to deploy the parachute. They were going to crash, and there was nothing he could do about it. Daylight began to dim and then darkness overcame him.

"SHIT. THIS LOOKS WORSE THAN my Christmas lights." Cai tried to unravel the cords and cables of his parachute with little success. They had got wrapped and twisted as they landed. It had been a rough landing that had scared Cai more than anything before. Not because they had nearly crashed to death, but because Shahin had been unresponsive for the last minute or so of the flight and was still unconscious as Cai worked at freeing both of them from the maze of cables.

After what felt like hours, Cai was finally able to rid himself of the cables. He knelt by his boyfriend and began unzipping and unbuckling the cumbersome wingsuit so he could reach flesh and bone. Shahin's breathing, however shallow, was a relief to Cai's ears, but the fact he was not responding to his calls or touch was worrisome. Cai peeled him out of the suit and flattened his ear against Shahin's chest. His heartbeat was strong and stable. He sighed.

"Sha, please say something." Gently, he shook him. Nothing. Shahin's skin was cold to the touch, but then again, they had just dropped from a very high mountain. His own fingers were still numb from the cold air. "Please, Sha. You're worrying me."

A tiny movement made his heart skip a beat. Shahin's bluish lips began moving as if attempting to say something. Cai held one of his hands between his and began rubbing it, trying to bring back some warmth to his skin.

"Cai?" His voice was weak, but it made Cai almost jump for joy. "Are we dead?"

A chuckle left Cai's lips as he took hold of Shahin's other hand and began massaging heat into it. "No, we're alive. You did your best to kill us, but fortunately failed."

Shahin opened his bright blue eyes and met Cai's. "I feel dead. Are you sure I'm alive?"

Cai couldn't handle it anymore. Putting decorum aside, he threw himself on top of his mate and hugged him. "You stupid man. You're sick, Sha, and you could have died. You could have killed us both. And for what?"

"You're suffocating me." The laughter belied his words, but Cai let him go and helped him sit up. It was very cold in that valley. Cai grabbed the wingsuit and draped it over Shahin's shoulders. "Did you like it?"

Exasperated, Cai bent forward and kissed Shahin. "You adorable, reckless fool," he whispered over his mate's lips. "Yes, it was amazing up to the part when you passed out while we were hurtling toward a very hard ground at sixty miles an hour."

Shahin looked around them, a freezing hand brushing Cai's cheek. "How did we not die?"

"I guess you taught me well, or maybe my survival instincts kicked in." Cai laid his hand on top of Shahin's. "When I realized you were out, I deployed my parachute and brought us down safely."

"You're kidding me." Shahin's eyebrows arched upward. "That's never been done. You told me you've never jumped before."

"I haven't—what do you mean, it's never been done?" The cold was beginning to seep through his clothes, making him shiver.

"Two people in a regular parachute. Super risky." His lips parted and his face softened, a hand over his heart. "How did you manage that?"

Cai's mind raced, looking for a rational answer, but couldn't find any. He had no idea how he had managed to do that. "We got lucky? I have no clue, Sha. I did drop you when we were close to the ground.

Accidentally. You may be a little sore tomorrow."

Shahin burst out laughing, holding his stomach and folding in two. "That's my Cai. Brave and humble. And a bit clueless. That's why I love you so much."

Not sure whether to be offended or gratified, Cai smiled. "I love you too."

The words had come out before he could stop them. He bit his lip. Of course, he loved the hawk-man. What was there not to love? But he didn't want to commit yet. Not out loud, even if inside him he knew—he was helplessly in love with his soul mate. Keeping that information under wraps served no rational purpose other than tricking himself into thinking he had the upper hand.

A gasp escaped Shahin's lips. "What did you just say?"

Cai lowered his eyes and bit his lip again. "I love you too." No point in hiding now. Everything was out in the open. He lifted his eyes to his mate and almost yelled, "I. Love. You. Do you understand? I love you, Sha, and you better not break my heart, ever."

Shahin drew him into his arms and held him there silently. Cai could feel the other man's heart beating through layers of clothing to join his own. It was exciting and wonderful to be in love, but terrifying as well. After a while, he pulled apart from his mate and looked him straight in the eyes. He needed to know the truth. The truth about this mysterious illness that was keeping him awake at night with worry. The truth about that day's strange events and

Shahin's cryptic words. His lover was keeping something from him, and it was time things came out in the open.

"What's going on, Sha? What are you hiding?"

Shahin didn't shy away from him this time. "I may be dying, love."

Cai's shoulders stiffened. "What do you mean, dying?"

"It's an old curse that plagues my species." Cai couldn't tell whether he was serious or trying to be funny. "I'm showing a lot of the symptoms."

With a hitch in his breath, Cai put a hand to his throat. "You have to go to a doctor." His voice was shaky and soft. "Please."

"It wouldn't do any good." Shahin shook his head, his shoulders slumping forward. Cai's eyes burned with the threat of tears. "It's a *cambiador* disease."

Cai's reaction surprised even himself. Anger bubbled up his throat until it exploded in words—words spat out, shot like bullets into an invisible target. "Bullshit! I'm taking you to my doctor even if I have to drag you there myself. I won't let you go without a fucking fight."

Shahin drew Cai against him again, holding him tightly as Cai slapped his back in anger and frustration. Why hadn't Shahin gone to the doctor the first time he got sick? Maybe then something could have been done. Why was he now threatening to leave him behind, just as he came to terms with loving this man more than he loved himself? How dare he get sick and leave him. No, he was going to make sure Shahin had a fighting chance. The man he loved was not going anywhere.

CHAPTER ELEVEN

MOMMY DEAREST

"**H**aven't you ever wondered?" Shahin sat in the corner of the crowded living room beside his sister, voice hushed so his mother wouldn't hear him. "Our father. Aren't you curious about him?"

Maya threw a worried glance in the direction of their mom. "Shh, Shahin. If Mom hears you, we're in trouble."

Shahin's familiar sense of prickly rebellion made his skin pucker in goose bumps. "Fuck. We're not little kids anymore, Maya. She can't tell us not to be curious about our own father." Maya stuck a finger in front of her lips, eyes nervously seeking the forever cranky figure of the Halcón matriarch. "Don't you want to know what he did to piss her off so much?"

"You never did before. What's changed?" Maya lowered her

voice even more.

Shahin shifted his glance to the floor. "I haven't been feeling good." Coming to terms with the fact that he would possibly die because he was in love with a full-human was not something he had been able to do yet. Admitting it to someone else, even less. "The story about interspecies relationships—"

Maya stiffened beside him. "Oh, my God. Are you telling me that you're sick because of your dating the full-human?" He nodded, a lump in his throat preventing him from speaking. The thought of dying was not a pleasant one, but the worst part was the thought of never seeing his love again, of wandering into whatever lay beyond this life and leaving Cai behind. "You have to stop seeing him, brother. Before it's too late."

There was no way he was going to stop seeing Cai. Not only was he irrevocably in love with him, but there was the ever-insistent pull of the soul mate. He laughed bitterly. "I'm screwed, no matter what I do. Even if I wanted to stop seeing Cai—which I don't—I would get sick from being separated from him."

"Are you sure he's your soul mate?" Her voice rose to a squeal. "How can you be sure?"

"What's this about a soul mate?"

Shahin's heart dropped to his stomach. His mother had stopped in her tracks and trained her laser stare on the two of them.

Shit. Just what I wanted to avoid.

He jumped to his feet, regretting it immediately. His muscles were still sore from the short but intense drop a few days ago with Cai. Morphing into his hawk had not been an easy feat lately, so he had given up trying. But he so wished he could just grow into his wings then and fly out of the house and away from the piercing eyes of his mother.

"I need some coffee," he said to no one in particular, heading to the kitchen as fast as he could. Mom tried to stop him, but he effectively managed to avoid her.

The kitchen was the only place he really liked in the family home. It was big and spacious and had a giant hearth-style oven that lent the room an aura of comfort he rarely got in that house. He opened the cabinet over the coffee machine and grabbed a mug. Something fell and rolled over the counter. *Eye drops? Who stores eye drops in the kitchen?* His mom, of course. Nothing his mother did ever made much sense. Including hiding the truth about his father. He was determined to find out who the man was. His sudden brush with mortality made him fully aware of that missing piece in the puzzle of his shifter life.

After pouring himself a cup of black coffee, he contemplated staying in the kitchen, but he knew there was no point in avoiding the inevitable forever. Coffee in hand, Shahin stepped into the living room again and almost walked into his mother.

"Did I understand correctly? That you've been feeling sick lately?

Weak and dizzy? Nauseous?" She was relentless.

"Mom, don't start. I've had the stomach flu, that's all." He tried to walk around her, but she blocked his way. He took a long drink to stop himself from saying something rude and almost choked on it. "I'll be fine."

With a finger stuck up in the air, she went on, "It's the curse, my son. You have to distance yourself from your full-human. It will kill you."

"I'm not leaving Cai, Mom. I love him and have no wish of giving him up because of a stupid story." He felt a little guilty since he now was almost 100 percent sure the story was true. It couldn't be a coincidence that he had been feeling increasingly worse the closer he got to Cai. "So, give up already. He's my soul mate, and I will stay with him, even if it kills me." And it probably would.

Two of his nephews ran to him and wrapped themselves around Shahin's legs. "Whoa, boys. You're going to make me spill this coffee on you." The two young boys giggled and ran away, chasing each other. "Your mom is going to kill you," he called after them.

"When are you going to settle down, Shahin? Find a nice girl from another flock and maybe have a couple of these fledglings?" What part of being gay didn't his family understand? He shook his head, thinking it better not to reply to his sister-in-law's irrational question.

Shahin lingered a while longer, but he could feel it, gnawing at him, begging him to go. Cai was calling him. He said his goodbyes and left in a hurry. The ride, which he normally loved, was too long that night. He was itching to shed his clothes and glue his body to Cai's, run hungry fingers over his hard muscles, and explore that delicious mouth with his. A shiver ran along his spine and he wiggled on his seat, his jeans suddenly uncomfortably tight. He pressed on the gas and the motorcycle sped down the road, a blur of movement under the light of the moon.

As soon as Cai opened the door, he cupped his nape and pulled him closer, his lips seeking his mate's with a desperation that defied reason. With Cai, he was as strong as he was weak. It was in the contradiction in terms that their love thrived. As he tasted his mate, Shahin's heart expanded and sang just as the nausea and dizziness returned with a vengeance. If only he could make his time with Cai last a little longer.

WAS IT POSSIBLE THE WEATHER was literally reflecting his mood? The low, gray clouds seemed to be following him and he half-expected the rain to start falling on his head at any moment. Shahin had collapsed in his arms again the night before. Weak, almost incoherent, Shahin had been too sick to do anything else than lie against him in bed, shivering under the covers. Cai knew he was hiding something, but couldn't imagine what. Despite Cai's insistence, Shahin refused to see a doctor, claiming there was nothing medicine could do for him. Having his usually vibrant and wild boyfriend lethargic and listless, cocooned within his arms, was too painful. He had to find out what was going on.

Now, as he stood before the door of Shahin's family home, he hesitated. The Halcón matriarch was not the motherly type. His own mother had been sweet and encouraging of both her kids, but Shahin's was caustic and so down on her own offspring, she made Lucifer look like a kindly patriarch. However, when all was said and done, she was most likely the one person who knew what was wrong with his lover.

"What the hell are you doing here, full-human?" The abrasive voice behind him could only belong to one person.

Cai turned around to face the short, unremarkable woman Shahin called his mom. She had been pretty at one time, Cai thought. There was a forgotten beauty behind the scowl and the razor-sharp blue eyes that homed in on Cai as if trying to melt him to the ground. Softness had long been replaced by a tough and prickly shell. Cai wondered how much of that was a defensive shield, but decided the barbs were there for attack purposes as much as for self-protection.

"Mrs. Halcón, good to see you again." He almost choked on his lie. His mother had always taught him to be polite even when talking to people who didn't deserve it.

"Bullshit! Save me the niceties. You're as glad to see me as I am to see you." Cai opened and closed his fists, struggling to stay calm. "What are you doing here where you know you're not welcome?"

Cai cleared his throat, stopping the words that climbed up before they left his mouth. He needed this woman to give him information about Shahin's state of health, and antagonizing her in any way wouldn't be the smart way to go. "I was wondering whether you could help me with something."

She cackled. "You must be delusional. What makes you think I'd be willing to help you with anything?"

He couldn't help it. The question bubbled to the surface. "Why do you hate me so much? I never hurt you in any way."

"You're a non-*cambiador*, a filthy full-human." The bitter woman spat the words as if the term itself burned her tongue. "I don't need any other reason to not like you. But you're also killing my son."

Cai stumbled backward a few steps. "What do you mean? How am I killing your son?"

She laughed again, crossing her arms and scanning him up and down. "Have you noticed how sick he is? How he shakes and faints? The way he's so weak, he can't change into his hawk?"

"That's why I came to you. I'm worried about him. He told me he's suffering from some shifter disease. A curse of some kind." Cai turned the palms of his outstretched hands upward, pleading. "I want to help him, but don't know how."

"You stupid human. *You're* killing him." She pointed an accusing finger in his direction. "You're the reason he's sick. It's the curse of the shifters. No cross-species matings allowed."

Cai's mouth fell open. What was she talking about? How come his boyfriend had never told him of such thing? Wouldn't Shahin have said something if that was true? Even before he finished the thought, he knew the answer—of course Shahin wouldn't have said anything. He wanted the relationship to continue. If he felt the pull as strongly as Cai did, there was no wish to fight it. It was too strong, too demanding. He remembered how ill he had felt when he tried to stay away from his lover for a few weeks.

"If you keep sleeping with my son, you'll end up killing him." The woman looked at him and he saw the hawk in her—the sharp tongue, the beady eyes, the curve of her neck as if poised to kill.

He swallowed the lump that had gathered in his throat. "I love your son and he loves me. We're soul mates."

"If you really loved my son, you'd leave him be so he can heal and be healthy again." Her voice had turned into a low growl. "Words are beautiful but empty if not backed up by deeds. You keep saying you love him and yet you kill him one day at a time, piece by piece, every time you make love to him, every time you touch him."

Something shattered inside him. Was that true? Was he the cause of Shahin's mysterious malaise? Was he poisoning his mate with his kisses, his caresses, his loving? It couldn't be. Or could it? Just a couple months ago he would have thought a man turning into a hawk an impossible, even ridiculous notion. He knew better now. It was hard to keep a clear mind about what was and wasn't real or true. What he had always thought to be reality had been far from it.

"I tire of your scent." Dismissing him as she would an annoying mosquito, she opened the front door and stepped inside. "Do the right thing and prove me wrong about full-humans." She closed the door behind her, leaving Cai alone on the porch, staring at the dark wood in shock.

Slowly he began to move. As if in a trance, Cai got in his car and drove home. He went up to his studio, slipped into his painting frock, and dove into the world of his art. Brush in hand, with each stroke he willed his thoughts away, his feelings, everything that at the moment caused him as much pain as joy. Cai wanted to forget the words Shahin's mother had spat in his face, but most of all he wanted to deny what his heart was telling him. He had to save his mate and that meant he had to do the one thing he couldn't bear—deny himself and Shahin of each other.

The anger and frustration growing inside him boiled to the surface with such intensity, he had to let it loose. A scream, guttural and agonizing, left his lips as he threw the brush at the canvas, paint splashing the floor in a rain of colorful pigments. How was he going to do the one thing that would tear him apart? How did you part with your heart? Leave your soul behind? How would he be able to live when the one who had brought him back from a dormant life was not there anymore?

He felt it at the same time he heard the doorbell ring. *Fight it, fight it.*

He had to protect Shahin, save him from what was making him sick. The pull thought otherwise and called him, yelled at him. Like the arrow in a compass, his heart pointed and pulled toward the door where his mate stood still, waiting and yearning for him. Shahin deserved an explanation, but Cai knew that if he opened that door, he would fall into his mate's arms again. If it was hard to resist the pull from afar; when they were together was impossible. He couldn't do that to his boyfriend, his love.

Resist it. You can do it.

The bell rang again and his legs responded automatically, moving toward the stairs, the invisible strings pulling him.

No! You can't go to him.

The bell rang a few more times. By then, Shahin must have wondered. He could feel Cai inside, just as Cai could feel his mate. Shahin knew he was inside the house, ignoring his call. Pain and doubt filled him and the weight of what he was doing pressed on him, suffocated him. Cai dropped to the floor, slumped over, and cried. He had finally met his soul mate and he had to let him go. Would the pain ever fade?

SHAHIN SHOOK OFF THE CONFUSION he felt and focused on the anger. Even though he had no clear target for the red-hot fury raging in him, he was determined to unleash it on somebody or something. Cai might be the one shutting him out, but deep down inside he knew there was more to that story than he had been made aware of. His soul mate was not the kind of man to finally admit his love and then run away. Something smelled rotten, and he was going to find out what.

"I don't care what you say, sis."

In an almost unprecedented sisterly gesture, Maya had invited him out for drinks. Shock didn't even begin to describe how he felt about it. They'd grown up together in that crowded, noisy chicken coop that was his family home, but they had never been close. He loved his sister—possibly more than anyone else in his family—but they had always led very separate lives; his sister was the obedient one, following Mom's every step and directions to a tee, while he ran the other way.

"You're being obstinate, Shahin." Maya took a swig of her cocktail, a strange concoction of greens and reds. The Christmas Devil, she called it. The holidays were around the corner and the bar was bathed in seasonal spirit already. "Mom will have your head for dessert if you don't stop."

Shahin hugged his glass of wine with his hands, swishing the red liquid around absentmindedly. "I'm doing it, Maya. I already contacted someone in Canada who knew Mom around the time you were born and promised him a pretty penny for information on our father."

Maya sighed. "It's your funeral, my brother. You always have to do everything in your power to piss off our mother." She laid a hand on his arm, and Shahin almost jumped in surprise. His family was not the touching kind. Sometimes he wondered whether his siblings kissed and hugged their own families when no one was around. "Are you feeling better?"

Since Cai had shut him out from his life, almost a week ago, he had not felt as sick. No nausea, and the dizziness had faded somewhat, but the pull was killing him. It was so bad, he sometimes would hide behind the trees in the back of Cai's house so he could be physically close to him and relieve some of the pressure their separation caused. Cai had to feel it too. How did he bear this deep, wrenching ache inside that stole every color from the world around him?

"I'm better, I guess." He hated to admit that his mother was right. "But I don't intend to let my love slip through my fingers just because of a stupid curse. I'll find a way even if it kills me."

With an unsure giggle, Maya dropped her hand and returned her attention to her drink. "And it probably will, Shahin. I wish you weren't so damned stubborn."

The familiar prickles of outrage assailed him. "Somebody has to. You guys just follow her like tiny chickadees with no will or thought."

Maya threw him a pained look, and he felt a twinge of regret.

He didn't want to hurt his sister. She was as much a victim in their mother's royal entourage as anybody else. Being the oldest and only surviving member of one of the first North American *cambiador* flocks, their mother was the bearer of lore and information about their species no one else could provide in the family. *Cambiadores* had spread throughout the world from their original and ancient nest in the warm coast of Andaluzia, in Spain, but like their full-human counterparts, some flocks had soon lost contact with each other, separated by space and circumstances. Even though many flocks regularly interacted at large family-type reunions, they still kept mostly to themselves, holding their stories and their secrets like valuable treasures they were not willing to share.

"Do what you want, brother. But in the end, we're the only family you have, and there aren't that many of us around anymore. You'll be a very lonely hawk if you keep pushing everyone away."

"I'll be a very lonely hawk anyway, sis." Shahin stood up and emptied the wine glass in one go. "I've always been alone and always will be."

Without a glance backward, Shahin walked away, dodging the other patrons and emerging into the cold night alone and without a coat. It didn't matter. The cold would do him good. It would distract him from the pain he felt inside, the emptiness left by Cai.

He walked the streets of town, hugging himself, and too distracted by his own thoughts to notice how cold it was. The air smelled like snow, but he walked on until his fingertips were frozen and turning blue. Startled, he realized he had walked all the way to Cai's neighborhood. He could see his mate's house at the end of the cul-de-sac, the darkness of trees framing the structure.

"No, I won't let it happen." Making a decision, he rushed down the street in the direction of Cai's place. He loved Cai and was very willing—however painful that'd be—to let him go if that's what he wanted. But he needed to hear the reasoning behind such a decision. He couldn't just let things go without talking to him.

Cai didn't answer the door. Shahin knew he was home. He could feel his presence as palpably as if he was standing in front of him. The pull didn't lie. He knocked again, harder this time.

"Open the door, Cai. Please, I need to talk to you." Nothing. In his mind, he could hear Cai's breathing. Their connection was getting stronger, more coalescent. "Please, Cai, I'm begging you. I won't touch you, I won't make you do anything you don't want me to do. I just want to talk to you."

After what felt like an eternity, he heard the clicking of the deadbolt. The door opened slowly and the face of his man appeared. Shahin had to use all his strength not to throw himself into Cai's arms. Instead, he smiled weakly and stepped inside, never taking his eyes from Cai. His boyfriend didn't look too good; there were dark circles around his eyes and Shahin could have sworn he'd lost weight since he'd last seen him.

"What are you doing here, Sha?" If he felt as tired as his voice sounded, Cai must not have slept properly in a few days. Shahin knew exactly how it felt. He hadn't been getting much sleep either. "I don't want you to get sick again."

Shahin's eyes widen. "Why would I get sick for being here?" A terrible suspicion rose in his mind. Had his mother talked to Cai about the curse? "Did you see my mom? Did she tell you—?" Cai's face was all the answer he needed. "And you believed her? She's a mean, bitter woman who will do anything to make me provide her with fledglings."

Cai's hazel eyes were wet and rimmed in red. "She was telling the truth, Sha. You've been getting increasingly sick since we've been dating. You can't even change into a hawk anymore."

All his instincts were telling him to go to Cai, to draw him into his arms and kiss him until he could erase the creases on his forehead and dry the tears in his eyes. But he had promised not to touch him. "I don't care, Cai. Even if it's true, that our love is killing me, I can't be without you. I rather die with you by my side than live forever without you."

"I can't let you do that, Sha." His voice trembled. He took a step back as if afraid they were too close. "I can't watch you die because of me."

Shahin wanted to yell, to stomp his feet like a spoiled child, hold his breath until he was purple. If only it were that simple. He took a deep breath, calmed himself down, and raised his eyes to Cai's again. "Did she also tell you that now that I met my soul mate, I'll never be able to mate with anyone else? That I may live a very long and very lonely life?"

Cai's eyes mirrored his surprise. "That can't be true, surely."

"Hawks are monogamous. They mate for life." Shahin took a step forward. "Shifters are no different. Once we meet our true soul mate, that's it for us. No more fucking around, Cai. You are *it* for me. Are you really going to let me live a life of solitude because you're afraid I'll die if I stay with you?"

Cai twisted his hands, his eyes searching Shahin's for a sign. He so wanted to hug him, to comfort him. It couldn't be easy coming to terms with him and his freaky family. Not only did he have to accept the fact that his boyfriend shared a body with a hawk, but now he had to digest another bit of outrageous information.

Cai sagged against the wall and slid to the floor, his hands covering his eyes. "My God, Sha. I don't know what to believe anymore. What to feel or what to do." Shahin restrained himself from crouching by him and doing what his body and heart were urging him to do. "I love you. That's the only thing that makes sense to me. The only real thing. I love you and don't want to see you suffer in any way."

"Then don't. I'll be fine as long as I'm with you." He waited, afraid of touching Cai and ruining everything.

Cai looked up and smiled, a few tears rolling down his cheeks and hanging precariously over his lips. "I need a fucking hug, Sha. Are you just going to stand there while I make a fool of myself?"

Shahin laughed, relief washing over him like cool rain. "I promised I wouldn't touch you. And I keep my promises."

With a sound that was a cross between a chuckle and a sob, Cai stretched out his arms in front of him. "Come over here, fool."

There was no need for further invitation. Shahin dropped in front of him and wrapped his arms around his mate, squeezing Cai's familiar body against his. He could smell Cai's subtle aftershave as he nuzzled against his lover's neck. It was good to be back where he belonged. Whatever the future held, they would face it together.

CHAPTER TWELVE

FAMILY SECRETS

Lyra stuffed a gigantic spoonful of pumpkin pie in her mouth. "Why isn't Shahin here with you?" The words were warped by her full mouth, and she had to repeat the question for Cai to understand.

"That's disgusting." Cai frowned as the orange contents of her mouth, fully visible as she talked, dripped onto the table. "He's at his family's. He'll come over afterward." Cai was already dreading it. Shahin seemed to always come back sicker every time he visited his mother, almost as if breathing in her noxious moods made him ill. But it was Thanksgiving and, good or bad, that was the only family Shahin had.

"Is his mom as bad as I hear?" Zack grabbed the spoon out of Lyra's hand and helped himself to some pie straight from the pan.

"Worse." Cai stared at his sister and her boyfriend and shook his head. "Have you guys ever heard of plates? Other people want to eat some of that pie. The same one you've been dipping your spit-infested spoon in."

As if to spite him, Cai's sister scooped a bit of pie with her fingers and licked it. "Our spit is like holy water." Zack chuckled. "And is Shahin feeling any better?"

Cai fell silent. It was one thing thinking about it, another saying it out loud. It needed to be said though. He couldn't avoid the obvious. "No. He has good days and then he gets worse again."

Lyra wiped her hands on a kitchen towel and came to hug her brother. "Is there a pattern to his ups and downs? Maybe he's allergic to something."

Yeah, me. He's allergic to his soul mate.

He trusted his sister implicitly, but how could he tell her his boyfriend could turn into a hawk and that he was the one killing him?

"He always seems to get worse after he visits his mom every week. It's her poisonous comments, I guess." He began putting some dishes away. He planned to have a second, more frugal dinner with Shahin later. If he was up for it.

With an expansive gesture, Lyra exclaimed, "See? There you have it. Something in his mother's house is making it worse—food he eats there, or maybe a pet. No one gets sick because of obnoxious comments." She had a point. If Cai was the reason for his illness, then why was he always sicker after being at his family's house? Was it possible something there was making things worse?

They sat in the living room, coffee mugs in hand and the fire in the hearth roaring. Lyra cuddled up on the sofa against Zack, and Cai wished Shahin was there with him.

"Zack, you still have some contacts in Canada, right?" A kernel of an idea popped in his head. Maybe he could help his mate find the information he was seeking about his enigmatic father. "Do you think you could find someone who may be able to track Shahin's father?"

Zack sat up and leaned forward. "Probably. Do you have a name?"

Cai shook his head. "No, just a place and a date. I know it's not much to go on, but he was married into a family with a very unusual name."

"I'll give my friend a call tomorrow and see what he can do." Zack set his mug down on the end table and hugged Lyra. "I think I'll have more pie."

Lyra and Zack waited for Shahin until after eleven, but he never came. They said their goodbyes and left. The house felt very empty all of a sudden as worry settled in. Why was Shahin not back yet? He normally came back from his home forays by ten at the latest. Where could he be? *It's Thanksgiving. He's spending more time with his siblings and their kids.* But he knew better. The Halcóns were not that kind of family. As much as Shahin loved his brother and sister, their relationship was not a close one like Cai had with his sister. Shahin wouldn't voluntarily spend more time with them than what he thought was expected of him.

Pacing to and from the window, Cai couldn't settle, worry growing inside him like an ugly and poisonous weed. *Sha, where are you?* He was not close. He would have felt him. *Call me, Sha.*

As if on cue, the phone rang. Cai ran to pick it up, tripping over the couch and almost landing on his face. The familiar number on the caller ID made him sigh in relief. "Sha? Where are you?"

"Sorry, love. I have some great news." He sounded excited. "I located my dad. That's why I'm late. I've spent the last two hours talking to someone in Canada."

Cai sighed again. He was okay. Better than okay—he sounded thrilled. "I was worried, Sha. But I'm happy for you. What did you find out?"

"Can you come to my place tonight?" They spent most of their time together at Cai's house since he often had to get up early to go to work. "I'm not feeling well enough to ride there."

Cai's chest contracted. Again. "Are you okay? You shouldn't be alone. I'm coming over now." Even before hanging up, Cai had grabbed his coat and keys, and ran out the door. Shahin's house was not far, a quick ten minutes from his place, but it felt like forever. He parked his Corolla in front of the house and ran up the few steps to the front door. Shahin rarely locked his door, something Cai often chided him for. As expected, the door was unlocked and Cai was able to enter immediately.

"Sha, where are you?" Cai yelled out for his mate while locking the door behind him. He heard a weak reply coming from the bedroom and he ran in its direction.

Shahin was lying in bed, propped up by a couple pillows, his dark eyelashes in stark contrast with the paleness of his skin. As Cai approached, he opened his eyes and a smile stretched his bluish lips. "Cai, you're here."

Even though the house was warm, Shahin was shivering. Cai rushed to his side, removed his coat, his shoes, and the rest of his clothes, and slid between the sheets next to his mate. Wrapping his arms around Shahin, Cai hoped he could warm up his mate with his body heat.

"You should have come home right away, Sha." Cai whispered the words into his mate's ear, blowing warm air onto the side of his face. "You're so cold."

"But I found my dad, Cai. I have an address and a phone number." He could barely open his eyes, and his voice came out weak and shaky. "We can call tomorrow."

Torn inside, Cai held him tighter. "Yes, we'll do that. But now you need to rest, Sha. Lean on me and sleep." Even sleep scared him, afraid as he was that one day Shahin wouldn't wake up. "I love you."

Shahin's slow breathing told him he had fallen asleep. Cai held him all night, not once closing his eyes. Every so often he'd kiss his lips, making sure his mate was still breathing. Fear controlled him, tensing his muscles and putting all his senses on red alert. He had never thought he'd love someone this much and know this strange type of agony—happiness mixed up with sadness in equal parts.

The morning came just as Cai was finally dozing off. The pressure of Shahin's body against his was a pleasant reminder of their love for each other, but also a warning of how tenuous his hold on life was right now. Shahin was warm and breathing steadily. Cai slipped out of bed, picked up his discarded clothes from the floor, and began dressing.

"What's the hurry?" Shahin's radiant blue eyes were open and trained on him. The redness framing them reminded him of how frail he had looked and felt the night before. Tears burned behind Cai's eyes, but he forced a smile into his lips. "Are you going to work already?"

"It's Black Friday. The studio is closed." He shook the pants he was holding to straighten them out. "Are you feeling better?"

"I'd feel a whole lot better if you dropped those jeans and joined me in bed." Shahin's wicked smile made every word sound sexy. Cai shivered. "Please."

Cai looked at the beloved face of his mate and frowned. "You were so sick last night, Sha. Do you really think you're up to it?"

With panache, Shahin flipped the bedcoverings off his naked body to prove how ready he was. "Can't be any more up to it than this." He winked.

His reaction to his mate was immediate and intense. Dropping the pants on the floor, he slipped out of his underwear and pounced on the bed beside Shahin, who laughed delightedly.

"I don't know how you do it, but I'm not complaining." Cai lowered his lips to Shahin's, pulling on his lower lip, his mate's snake bite caught between his teeth. He licked it, tasting the mix of metal and Shahin's intoxicating flavor. "I love you, hawk-man."

Later, as they lay side by side in the aftermath of their lovemaking, they talked in whispers entangled in each other's arms. Shahin was still excited about what he had discovered the night before and couldn't stop talking about it. Cai wanted to be excited for him—was, in fact—but he feared what a bad reception from his father would do to Shahin's spirits. He hadn't flown in weeks, either as a hawk or in his wingsuit. Flying was the one thing that brought his mate happiness. Cai liked to think he did too, but deep in his heart, he knew that Shahin needed to fly to be truly in touch with life. It was part of who he was. If on top of his already weakened spirit, it turned out his father didn't want to talk to him, it may well be catastrophic.

"When are you planning on calling him?" Cai asked.

"Later today." Shahin sat up, supported on one elbow, and looked at Cai intently. "Will you be there with me when I do?"

Cai's heart swelled. "Are you sure you don't want to be by yourself?"

Shahin laughed. "Fuck no. I want my soul mate to be there,

holding my hand so I don't pass out with anxiety."

"You? Pass out? Come on, you jump off cliffs for fun." Cai chuckled and kissed his cheek.

"That's nothing compared to talking to the man who gave me life and then took off running." The smile left his face and his eyes lost focus. "God knows what he's going to say—"

Cai brushed his hand over his mate's chest in a caress. "Whatever he says, you know I love you and I'll be here for you, right? You've lived your whole life without him, you don't need him."

Eyes focused again, Shahin lifted the corner of his mouth in a smile. "I'm just curious about him, that's all. And why my mother never even mentions his name."

In need of a good cup of coffee, Cai swung his legs over the edge of the bed and got up. "Time for some coffee and breakfast. Do you have any food in this house?" Shahin was not the best housekeeper in the world. He kept the house tidy but devoid of a lot of necessities and luxuries. He had no television, no radio, and often no food in the refrigerator. Cai suspected he spent very little time at home, choosing to fly or ride his motorcycle for entertainment. Now that they were together, Shahin spent most of his time at Cai's place.

"There may be a loaf of bread and maybe some butter." It didn't sound too promising. "But I do have coffee."

The house was warm even though there was no carpet on the floor as Cai walked barefoot and naked to the kitchen, leaving

Shahin still in bed. He opened the cabinet over the coffee machine and found several coffee capsules but no sugar or cream. *Black it is.* He filled two cups with the delicious-smelling brew and then opened the fridge to find the promised loaf of bread and butter. He slipped two slices into the toaster and waited for it to pop.

Shahin came up from behind him, stealthy as a cat, and pressed himself against Cai, pinning him to the cabinet. "You smell delicious." Shahin's nose was nestled in the crook of Cai's neck and wreaking havoc with his senses.

"It's the coffee. Not me." Cai chuckled softly, hardening against the wood of the cabinet. "If you don't stop soon, I may end up having sex with this furniture."

Shahin laughed and pressed himself even harder against him, his arousal rubbing against Cai's buttocks. "Should I be jealous then? Is the cabinet as hard as I am now?"

A little breathless, Cai laughed. "Well, it is made of wood. Literally." Pushing his mate, he spun around until he was facing his lover. A gasp left his lips as their bodies touched again. "But I so much prefer yours."

The coffee was left on the countertop until it was cold and the toast was forgotten. Who needed sustenance when they had each other?

SHAHIN HAD LONG HUNG UP the phone, and yet, he still held it to his ear as if expecting to hear something else. Cai stared at him, his eyebrows knitted together. "What happened? What did he say?"

His father had just dropped a bomb on him. Not the one he was half-expecting. He hadn't told him he'd left them because he couldn't stand his kids and his wife. Nothing was mentioned about how he might have wanted a new family, a new life. He had indeed alluded to the fact that living with his mom had not been easy and that the fact both she and all three children were shifters had made his life just a bit more complicated—not to mention hard to swallow.

"My father's name is Theo. Theo Mathison." Shahin was not totally out of his trance, his mind still replaying his father's words. "He's been living in Alberta for the past twenty years."

Cai, sitting next to him on the couch, pressed a hand on his thigh, encouraging him to go on. "You look a bit daunted. What did he say?"

After their lovemaking, they had taken a shower together, gotten dressed, and driven in Cai's car to his place. They had been starving and Cai had wisely suggested they put something in their stomachs before facing the possible shocking news. Shahin hadn't fought him. Cai prepared one of his simple but satisfying meals, and they ate together in the breakfast nook, sitting across from each other in silence. Shahin had too much on his mind and Cai respected him enough not to interrupt his thoughts.

"My mother has been lying for years."

Shahin knew Cai was not a fan of the Halcón matriarch, but he still seemed surprised. "What do you mean? Lying about what?"

Shahin put the phone down on the end table and brushed a hand over his face with a groan. "About pretty much everything. And not just to me, but to the whole flock."

"What about?"

"Old lore about shifters… how cross-species mating will hurt you." Cai's expression went from confused to outraged in a blink of an eye. "Yeah, she's been lying about me getting sick because I'm with you."

"How can you be so sure? What did he say exactly?"

Shahin was still having a hard time digesting what his father had said. "Theo Mathison is a full-human."

"What? But your mother—"

"Exactly. She's been lying to us. She lived and mated with a full-human for years. They had children together, and yet she never once became ill because of it." The anger ate him inside out. How could his mother, his own flesh and blood, be so deceitful that she was willing to propagate such a terrible lie to keep him away from Cai? How many other cross relationships in the flock had she ruined with that lie?

Cai held his hand. "Then why have you been getting so sick since we started dating?"

Shahin hadn't thought about that. He had no idea. Maybe he had indeed contracted some kind of bug. All he knew was that his relationship with Cai had nothing to do with it. And however great the news was, it didn't take away from the fact that his own mother had been lying to him and his family for too long.

"I don't understand half of it. My mother never ceases to amaze me." Shahin scratched his head, puzzled and heartsick. "What exactly did she accomplish by lying to all of us? What does she have against full-humans? I mean, she freaking fucked one for years." Anger was growing and festering in his chest. What right did his mother have to withhold his right to be happy with his soul mate? At least she had been honest about that story. There was no mistaking the pull between Cai and him. She must have never imagined he would find his in a full-human or she would have never said anything.

"Sha, you've been sick. Don't get all stressed about this." Cai was still holding his hand, anchoring and comforting him. "Let's instead celebrate the fact you're not dying because we love each other. That's something, right?"

Shahin smiled, a deep sigh escaping his lips. "You're right. Of course, you're right." He leaned over and tasted his lover's lips. "Let's celebrate. What do you want to do?"

Cai smiled. "I have an idea. Come on." Shahin followed his mate up the stairs and into his studio. He hadn't entered the room since his first night in the house. The look of hurt on Cai's face when he found out he'd been inside without his permission still haunted him. Shahin didn't want to make the same mistake again. "I've been meaning to share this with you, but—"

When the door opened, Shahin's heart drummed a little faster. Even though they had been intimate for a while now, Cai had yet to trust him with whatever that small room meant to him—which judging by his reaction all those weeks ago was a lot. The door opened to reveal what he had already seen: a small room, painted in a soft yellow, framed on one side by a whole wall of almost floor-to-ceiling windows. The canvases that filled the room, some leaning against the walls and furniture, a couple of them on easels, were covered in mostly bright-colored paintings—mostly abstract, color combinations with no particular or obvious shape. A few showed more concrete forms, identifiable bodies or silhouettes. One, on an easel bathed by the sunshine coming through the windows, was covered in a white rag stained with so many hues, it looked like fireworks had taken residence there.

"I know I got really shitty with you that day when you came in here while I was at work."

Shahin rushed to respond, worried that Cai might still be upset about it. "I'm so sorry I did that. I had no right—"

Cai laid a hand on his shoulder and shook his head. "No reason to apologize. I was the one who overreacted. I'm a bit sensitive about this room and what it means to me." He pulled Shahin against his side and swept an arm in front of him. "I wanted to be an artist when I was younger, but never believed I was good enough. When my mom got sick, I felt that my dream of becoming a full-time artist was ridiculous, even a little dangerous."

"Dangerous? How could that be?"

"I was broke like most artists are, picking up an odd job here and there. You can attest my knack for cooking to the time I worked as kitchen help at a local fancy restaurant." Cai laughed. "But with my mom sick, her health insurance not being able to cover all her medical expenses, and my sister still in college I realized I had to step up to the plate and get a well-paid job. A real job, like my father always said."

Shahin's heart burst with sympathy and tenderness toward his soul mate. "You gave up on your dream to help your family?"

Cai shook his head. "It was not totally unselfish. I figured I needed to help myself too. I was living in an awful apartment that was more like a hovel than a home, my car was so old I was never sure I'd make it there, and I skipped more meals than what was healthy for anyone. I felt I needed to make a change. So, I did."

Shahin drew his mate into his arms and kissed him. "I hate that you felt you had to give up on what you loved."

"My mom was not happy with me. She had always encouraged me to follow my dreams wherever they'd take me." Cai's voice trembled a little at the mention of his mother. "But I managed to convince her and myself that I was not really giving up on it, I was just using my talent and my love for art in a different way. One that paid better."

Shahin held him tight and allowed him a few moments of silence. He had learned early on in their relationship that talking about his mother was always difficult for Cai. He was often a bit jealous of the obvious love between mother and son considering his own mother could make a demon blush.

Cai pulled apart and pointed at his paintings. "I want to share this room with you. And my work." He took a few steps toward the rag-covered canvas. "After my breakup with Jack, I felt empty." Shahin cringed. He couldn't help but feel uncomfortable any time Cai's earlier boyfriends were mentioned. "That's not true. I was feeling empty way before that. The breakup just gave me the courage to do something about it."

Shahin watched with fascination as Cai began peeling the cloth from the canvas.

"This room is where my true heart is, my feelings, my heartaches." Cai stopped for a moment. "Until you showed up in my life, I kept all these feelings bottled and locked away in this room. I didn't allow anyone to see these paintings because if I did, it would be like standing naked and vulnerable in front of a crowd." He blinked, shaking his head again. "I know it sounds stupid—"

In one long stride, Shahin was beside him. "Not stupid at all. I totally get it. Don't apologize for how you felt. Never apologize for that."

"Anyway, I wanted you to be part of this, be privy to my full heart and soul." With a pull, he removed the cloth from the painting. "I've been working on this for a few weeks now. It's how I feel about us."

An explosion of blues in every shade from the pale pastels to the darkest midnight blues star-burst from the center to the outside edges of the canvas. It was peaceful and exciting all at the same time, a hint of sadness here and there where the blue darkened to purples, and a beating heart in the middle—a living, bursting-with-love red heart.

"This is us." Cai stepped aside as if afraid of Shahin's reaction.

Speechless and with emotion threatening to break free from his very being, Shahin reached out for his mate and drew him in for an embrace. "I love you so much it scares me sometimes." He crushed his lips to Cai's, trying to breathe him in, making him part of his own body, his soul. "I love it, Cai. Love everything about it. And love that you shared this part of yourself with me. Thank you."

Their lips met again, standing in front of the windows and lit by the rays of the sleepy sun. He may not have been able to turn into his hawk in a while and flown the skies, but within Cai's loving arms he had been flying high anyway. And for now, that's all he needed. It was perfection.

CHAPTER THIRTEEN

TINSEL & POISON

A smile crept onto his lips as he watched Ted from the corner of his eye, balancing on top of a short stepladder and stringing tinsel across the ceiling of the studio. Eliza, their coworker and Christmas expert extraordinaire, had somehow managed to recruit his tall and not-too-limber friend to help her decorate the office for the holidays. Ted teetered precariously on the edge of the ladder's top step, failing miserably at attaching the slippery garland to the popcorn ceiling tiles. Cai couldn't help but bursting out in laughter.

"Keep laughing," Ted muttered, the red garland falling from his hand again. "You'll be next on this ladder."

"Dream on, tinsel-boy." Cai was in high spirits that morning. Shahin was in the best health since he had first taken ill. The simple knowledge that he was not the one causing his illness made him insanely happy as well. "Bad enough I'll have to decorate my own place after work today." His sister had been emphatic about it. She was coming to his place around six and they were having a deck-the-halls party.

"I'll bring the booze, you provide the cookies," she had said. "Zack says he'll bring his appetite."

When he left Shahin that morning, the hawk-man had mentioned he felt well enough to fly. Cai couldn't be happier for him, knowing how much the hawk meant to his mate. He stole a glance toward the clock on his screen. It was almost lunchtime and Shahin should be getting back from his foray into the wild. They had decided to meet for lunch and Cai was itching to gaze at his lover's infinite eyes.

"Lyra is making you do it?" Ted stepped down and crouched to pick up the rogue garland from the floor. "She hasn't changed much since her teens, has she?"

Cai laughed. "No, she hasn't. Bossy and determined as always."

He remembered a time though when she had lost the spark. After their mom died, there were days when he worried about her sister's state of mind. Her usual exuberant, often unfiltered personality had been muted—or maybe snuffed out altogether. Even though his heart had been bleeding, he had to hold it together for his sister, making sure she didn't slip into the kind of depression it was almost impossible to crawl out from. In the end, she pulled through, her ever pushy and effervescent nature bubbling to the surface once again. It was about that time she had met Zack, who had the same soothing effect on her that Shahin had on Cai.

"Do you want to come over?" Selfishly, he hoped Ted would turn the offer down. Ted was his best friend, and he usually participated in the family's yearly ritual, but Shahin was coming, and Cai wanted to focus all his attention on his mate.

"Thank you but no. As much of a sucker for punishment as I am, two decorating duties in one day is more than I can stand." Ted let out a loud victory hoot as the garland was finally secured to the ceiling. "Shit, I thought that blasted tinsel was never going to stick."

"Well, I'm going off to lunch." Cai closed his laptop and gathered his gloves and scarf from one of his desk drawers. "Meeting with Sha. Want to come?"

Ted laughed as he stepped off the ladder. "Fuck, no. Sitting there watching you guys making googly eyes at each other? No, thank you. It's like watching a Hallmark movie live."

Cai put on his trench coat, wrapped the scarf around his neck, and waved. "Heading to get my happy-ever-after." Ted made a gagging sound and Eliza laughed from the other side of the office as he left the studio.

It was unusually cold for Virginia, a couple degrees negative, but the snow refused to fall. The skies were bright and cloudless, and the sun reigned over the landscape. Cai's breath came out almost solid in heavy globs of mist as he rushed toward the restaurant where he was meeting his mate. The pull spotted him before his eyes could, the insistent tug on his body and his heart. He sped up.

Shahin was already sitting at their usual table, a small booth in a corner, as private and cozy as you would get in a public place. Cai's blood pumped through his veins like wild river rapids, crushing against the rocks, lapping at the river banks. His lover's face had a glow he had not seen in a while. His skin was back to its normal tanned shade, a pinkish blush tinting his cheeks and a glimmer shining in his brilliant eyes.

Cai slid over the bench across Shahin, who immediately held his hand over the table. "Hello, gorgeous." He winked, his old wild self totally restored. Cai smiled, happy and relieved that he was finally feeling like himself again. Was it possible his illness had been totally psychosomatic? "I thought you'd never come."

Holding his hand, Cai brought it to his lips and kissed it. "I missed you."

Shahin laughed out loud. "Control yourself, lover. We're in public." His smile belied his words, and Cai was certain his mate wouldn't hesitate to throw him over the table and make love to him, audience be damned.

Cai let go of his hand and smiled. "I gather the flight went well." Shahin didn't have to say it. It was obvious in his smile, the twinkle in his eye, the blush across his face. He had been able to morph into his hawk. "You look—revitalized."

"You have no idea," Shahin whispered with a wink. "We should have met for lunch at your place or a hotel so I could show you how alive I feel right now."

The server came to take their order, and Cai covered his lap with the napkin, hoping no one would notice how Shahin's words affected him. It was going to be a long afternoon at work, his mind undoubtedly never straying too far from his lover.

"How did it go?" Might as well make conversation and try to distract himself from the tightness in his pants.

"Amazing. I had almost forgotten how it feels to fly up in the sky, above the world, the cold wind holding and blowing along your body to keep you floating and moving." His eyes had glazed over as he spoke, and for a brief moment, Cai was jealous of Shahin's hawk, of the air that lifted and caressed him, the expanse of the open skies that called his lover with the power of a siren. "Serendipity. I wish I could share it with you."

Cai threw his head back, laughing. "Well, that didn't go too well the last time." Shahin laughed with him. "But I'm so happy you were able to do it again. I know how much it means to you."

The food was served and they chatted about everything and nothing in particular for a while. Shahin felt like home to Cai, a feeling he had never felt with anyone before. Being with him was both exciting and calming, a sense of comfort and joy you could only experience with a certain perfection.

"Are you ready for the deck-the-halls torture this evening?"

"Are you kidding me? I wouldn't miss it for the world. Mostly because I'm pretty sure Lyra would hunt me down and kill me if I didn't show up." Shahin closed his hands around his neck and stuck his tongue out. "Your sister is so different from you."

Cai smiled and took a bite of his sandwich. "Yeah, she takes after my dad." The man who had not been able to handle things after their mom's death, putting some distance between them as a buffer from painful memories. Cai couldn't understand and probably never would, but he had long accepted his father's decision to move away from the ones who loved him the most. "Be prepared. She's like a colonial overseer. If she had a whip, she'd use it."

"Should I bring anything?" Shahin licked his thumb and Cai's gut tightened again. Noticing his reaction, his mate licked it again, this time slower, his eyes searching Cai's.

Cai gulped and straightened the napkin on his lap. "You're bad." *But I love it.* "You may want to bring a change of clothes. I put all your stuff in the washer before I left."

Shahin smiled wickedly and moistened his lips with his tongue. "What do I need clothes for? I have no intention of wearing anything after your sister leaves."

Cai laughed, not sure whether to feel uncomfortable or elated.

"You're wicked, Sha."

Soon, Cai had to go back to work. Shahin kissed him hard and long in the narrow alley between the buildings, sliding a hand to the front of Cai's pants as if to assure himself of his lover's reaction to him. Seeming satisfied, he smiled and left Cai adjusting his trench coat around himself before following him into the street. The day already seemed to stretch forever in front of him.

True to her word, Lyra was at his door by six o'clock on the dot. Zack, standing beside her, balanced a huge box of decorations in his arms while his sister held a wine bottle in one hand and a plastic container in the other.

"We're going to raise the roof," she declared, stepping into the house and barking like a dog. Zack gave Cai a commiserating look. "Where's your boyfriend? He *is* coming, right?"

Cai ran to Zack's aid and relieved him of the heavy box. "He'll be here. He had to go see his family first. He hasn't been to their house in a couple of weeks." Since finding out his mother had been lying to them all. Cai wondered what Shahin was going to say to the Halcón matriarch. He was hoping he didn't choose today of all days to do it. Cai was looking forward to a stress-free evening in the company of the two people he loved the best. There was no way Shahin would come out unscathed from such a conversation with his family viper. Better left to another day.

Lyra immediately started removing items from the box while

Zack poured everybody a glass of wine and opened the container with cookies.

"Did you actually bake?" Lyra was not known for her domestication.

"Hell, no. I bought them in town. Who do you think I am? Martha fucking Stewart?" *Typical.* He snickered and stole a cookie from the box. "Let's eat less and work more."

He sat on the edge of the couch and began pulling garlands and baubles from the box and staging them on the table. He hadn't bought a Christmas tree yet. For some reason, he wanted to buy it with Shahin. He felt stupid just thinking about it, but the desire to share that family moment with him was there nevertheless.

When the doorbell rang, Cai jumped to his feet. It was Shahin, he knew. Lyra got to the door first, wine glass in hand and a green garland wrapped around her neck like a scarf. Cai had to stop himself from racing her to the door.

"Thank you for gracing us with your presence finally, your hotness." Cai heard his boyfriend laughing before he saw him. "Join the fun."

Not able to wait any longer, Cai crossed the space between them and drew him into his arms. "How did it go?"

Shahin was a little pale, the previous glow gone. "The usual shit," he bantered, placing a kiss on Cai's cheek. "My mom, the world's biggest bitch." Cai cringed at the term. He would have never in a million years have called his own mother that. But he could see how it was so very appropriate with Shahin's mom.

"But you're okay, right? You didn't have *the* talk with her, did you?" They walked hand in hand to the kitchen to help themselves to some wine.

"God, no. That talk will have to wait until I have all my strength back. That woman can suck the life out of me." He smelled the wine and sighed. "I need this. Good wine and good company. My mother's coffee is amazing, but it sours because of her moods." He took a swig. "So what am I supposed to do?"

"Talk to the slave driver there." Cai pointed at his sister, who was enthusiastically giving orders to her boyfriend. "Good luck."

Zack looked at them and smiled. "All right. Now that we have the whole family together, it is time," he said cryptically. Lyra threw him a side glance.

"What are you talking about, Zack?" Cai had no idea what his sister's boyfriend was up to. Zack was always kind of quiet, especially compared to his girlfriend. A patient and kind man who totally got and complemented Lyra's sharp, sarcastic humor and strong personality.

Cai stood by Shahin, more than a little curious. Zack had gone down on one knee before Lyra who, for once, seemed to have been robbed of her power of speech.

"My dear, abrasive Lyra." Cai and Shahin chuckled, and Lyra looked outraged. Zack dug into his pocket and removed a small square black box. "I figured since we haven't killed each other yet after all these years of dating, we might as well get married." He opened the box to reveal a small diamond ring. "Lyra Banes, will you be my wife?"

The room fell silent for a few moments. Cai held his breath as his sister took her time to respond. She looked as if she was stunned by the proposal. For once, Zack had truly caught her off guard and managed to surprise her. Shahin squeezed his arm and smiled at him.

"Well? Are you going to answer me anytime soon? You can't possibly tell me you've never thought of us tying the knot." Zack thrust the tiny box toward her, urging her to accept it. "It's not exactly Elizabeth Taylor size, but it's a fucking diamond."

Lyra snapped out of her trance and threw herself at Zack's neck, yelping. "Of course I'll marry you, my sweet idiot. Today, tomorrow, whenever." Their lips locked in a kiss.

To his surprise, Cai felt tears of joy burning in his eyes. His mother would have loved Zack, and this proposal would have made her so proud. In fact, he was certain his mom would also have liked Shahin, with his good looks and wild personality. He could almost hear her. "That's a wild creature you have there, my son. Take good care of him, and he'll take good care of you." *I will, Mom. I most certainly will.*

THE EMOTIONAL IMPACT OF ZACK'S proposal might have been more than what he could handle in his state of convalescence. He felt dizzy and shivers assailed his body shortly after Lyra said yes. Nausea brewed in his stomach and began its climb up his throat. Was the sickness coming back? He had felt so much better for the past couple weeks that he'd come to believe he was out of the woods. It appeared he had jumped to conclusions too fast.

Zack and Lyra had left once the house decorations passed her strict expectations—at least, as much as they had managed to decorate that evening. After teasing Cai all day, he was not surprised his boyfriend was in a rush to get in bed with him. Shahin had also waited impatiently for this moment all day, but now that it was here his body refused to cooperate. As Cai undressed him, one tantalizing layer after another, Shahin struggled to keep steady on his feet, the room wavering and moving around him as if turned into liquid. The faintness weighted on his eyes and more than once he had to fight to keep them open. His boyfriend had disrobed and stood stark naked in front of him, his lovely body inviting his for their familiar sensual dance. He stumbled and braced himself on Cai's shoulders.

"What's wrong? Are you not feeling good again?" Cai's smile of a moment before was replaced by a frown of worry. "Are you sick again, Sha?"

Shahin dropped on the edge of the bed, his head swimming and his stomach threatening to empty itself onto the floor. "Sorry, Cai.

I'm not feeling too good."

"I thought you were doing better." Cai sat next to him, holding his hand.

"Me too. I guess we were both wrong."

Cai stood up suddenly and began collecting their clothes from the floor. "We're going to the hospital." Shahin opened his mouth to protest. "No arguing. We know it's not the curse, so it has to be something medical. We should have done this a long time ago. I'll help you get dressed."

Soon, Cai had helped him to his car, and they were on their way to the nearest hospital. He felt miserable. If before he had thought he was dying because of his forbidden relationship with Cai, this scared him even more. He had always been healthy. Shifters often were, being mostly immune to human and bird diseases. He caught the occasional mild cold and he had contracted a mild case of chicken pox as a kid. He had never had any serious illness other than scrapes and cuts, stitches and broken bones from being too wild, too much of a daredevil. This scared him witless. He didn't know how to react to a human disease, one that may not have a cure, or worse, one with a cure that would change him forever.

Eyes closed, unable to move much without causing a wave of wretched nausea, Shahin leaned his head against the headrest and willed himself to think of the open skies. Cai kept mumbling under his breath, cursing at traffic lights, and driving much faster than he normally did.

After Cai parked the car, he helped Shahin out of the car, his shoulder supporting his mate, as he stumbled to the ER's main doors. The staff jumped into action as soon as they saw him coming through the automated doors, pale as a ghost and barely able to stand. They took him to a stretcher in a flurry of activity, leaving Cai behind in the waiting room looking forlorn and scared.

"Cai. I want my boyfriend with me." His voice was weak and he couldn't be sure the medical staff had heard him.

"Sir, we have to check you first." It was a female nurse. She held his hand as they pushed the stretcher through the hospital hallways. "I promise I'll call him in as soon as I can."

She proceeded to ask him all kinds of questions, shot at him with the speed of a machine gun. He couldn't keep up with it, his eyes refusing to open and his body shaking with uncontrollable shivering. Shahin wanted Cai beside him, holding him and telling him everything was going to be all right. That they were going to be all right.

THE LAST TIME CAI HAD spent this much time in the waiting room of a hospital ER was shortly before his mom died. The space had been decorated tastefully with exquisite works of art and pale soft furnishings to infuse those who waited with a sense of calm, a sense of hope. Cai was always sensitive to the beauty of his surroundings, and normally he'd be fascinated by the great pieces adorning the white walls and placed strategically in more private corners where people were likely to retire to have a good cry. Today, the art had no effect on him at all. His whole body tensed up with fear and doubt, memories of his mother dying in that very hospital flooding his mind and taking a firm grip on his heart. What if Shahin didn't make it? What if the blurry figure on a stretcher being pushed by nurses through the doors was the last he'd see of his lover? His soul mate.

"Are you here with Mr. Halcón?" The young nurse cocked her head to look at him. He hadn't heard her approach, his head buried in his hands as he sat. He looked up, his heart fluttering in his chest. "You're his husband, right?"

Confusion clouded his brain. Husband? What was she talking about? Then he remembered their ruse weeks ago when Shahin had been hurt by the owl. The nurse looked vaguely familiar. "Sorry. Do I know you?"

The nurse—Anne, according to her name tag—laughed softly. "I remember you from the last time Mr. Halcón was here."

"Yes, I'm his husband. How is he?" He was not going to fight the convenient lie, and if they asked for proof, he'd cross that bridge when he got there. "Can I see him?"

Anne pointed at the doors leading to the ER main ward and

he followed her. "Yes, I'll take you to see him. He's doing all right. We've flushed most of the poison from his system, I think."

Cai stopped. *Poison? What is she talking about?* "What do you mean?" Was he hallucinating? Had he really heard her say what he thought she said?

"He was poisoned," she said, nudging him to resume their walk. "I'll let the doctor explain it to you. We've called the police. They should be here very soon."

If time had been dragging at a sluggish speed until then, it now had taken on a nightmarish nature. Poisoned? Who in heaven's name would do that to Shahin? And why? He followed the nurse obediently throughout the hallways until they reached the small windowed room where Shahin slept. Cai stopped again, watching him from outside the window. Tubes stuck out from many parts of his body and connected to machines—some of which Cai recognized, others he didn't. The tortured, dead pale expression on Shahin's face had been replaced with peace. He lay in the narrow bed, his whole face relaxed into the sweet oblivion of sleep.

"Come in. I'll go call the doctor and tell him you're here." She rushed out and left him in the small room with the man who meant the world to him.

Cai pushed a chair closer to the bed and sat down. Leaning forward, he held his mate's hand over the white blanket. Gently, almost fearfully, he rubbed his thumb over Shahin's knuckles, the tears and sobs gurgling dangerously close to the surface.

"You've scared me, Sha. I thought I lost you. Again." A lone tear rolled down his cheeks, which he wiped away with the back of his other hand. "You keep doing this to me. If I didn't love you so much, I'd kill you myself."

"Better be careful with what you say, buddy." Cai turned his face toward the voice. A doctor was leaning against the doorway, looking curiously at him. "Your husband was poisoned and the cops will be looking for the one who did it. The husband is always the first suspect."

Outrage replaced the tears in his eyes. "What poison? What are you talking about? He's been sick off and on for a few weeks now."

"Sorry. Didn't mean to accuse you of anything, just stating a fact." He walked closer to them and sat on the edge of the bed, facing Cai. "Did you say this is not the first time it's happened?"

Cai told him all about the many times he had to hold Shahin while he retched or shook violently through the night, his weakness, his paleness, the bluish color of his lips and the dizzy spells. A weird sense of relief washed over him, as if sharing the many times he had feared for his lover's life for the past weeks lightened the load. Or maybe got them closer to the truth.

"Well, someone has been slipping him some tetrahydrozoline." The doctor might as well have spoken in Chinese. The word sounded vaguely familiar, but he couldn't quite place it. The doctor took the hint. "Eye drops. Someone has been poisoning him with eye drops.

Do any of you use them at home?"

"You're kidding me, right? Eye drops?" Cai stiffened his back. "No, we don't have them in the house, but how would that be poisonous enough to make him so sick?"

"Common mistake. The compound is totally harmless unless ingested. Considering you say this has happened more than once, I'm willing to guess this was not accidental. Someone was trying to harm your husband." The doctor stood up and turned around to check on Shahin. "He's sleeping peacefully, and all his vitals are normal. He'll be fine as long as he doesn't get poisoned again. Eventually, this could kill him."

Who could possibly be poisoning Shahin? He didn't have any coworkers that could be holding a grudge against him, or even friends to speak of. Cai realized for the first time that for someone as wild as Shahin was, he was also a pretty lonely guy. His family was all he had, and God knew that was nothing to brag about.

His family. The idea hit him, heavy and absurd, but possible nevertheless. What if someone in his family had been poisoning him? Shahin was the middle child and by far the most rebellious of all the Halcóns, but like all the other members of the family he had a vital role in the hugely successful family business. He was in charge of everything cyber, from marketing to website design, and partaking of a very generous cut in the company's profits. With him out of the way, some other member of his family would take his place and take over the money. Was it possible that anyone in his family was that greedy? That evil?

With the arrival of the police, Cai was not able to think about it anymore. The police officers had hundreds of questions—some of which he couldn't answer—and they kept at it until Shahin finally began regaining consciousness.

"Sha." Cai ran to his side. "How do you feel?" He held Shahin's hand against his chest, hoping he could feel the joyful beating of his heart.

Shahin opened his eyes slowly, the ocean blue of his eyes shining through. "Am I dead?"

He couldn't hold it anymore. His chest was bursting with a mixture of joy and fear, threatening to explode at any time. *Damn the audience!* Cai molded his lips to Shahin's in a desperate kiss, wanting to inhale him, make him a part of him, never to lose him, never to part.

"I love you," he whispered for Shahin's ears only.

They feasted in each other's eyes for a moment longer until Shahin's gaze wandered behind Cai. "Why the cops?"

It took a while to explain everything to his mate. Cai sat on the edge of the bed, never letting go of Shahin's hand, and went over every detail of the conversations he'd had with both the doctor and the police. Shahin's face changed from one of blissful peace to an angry grimace, his hand tightening inside Cai's grip.

When Cai was finished, Shahin looked over his shoulder and

talked directly to the officers. "I won't be pressing charges."

Cai looked up in surprise. "What do you mean? Of course you're pressing charges when we find out who did this to you." A thought dawned on him. He lowered his voice. "You know who it was, don't you?" Shahin nodded, his eyes fluttering toward the cops. "Can you give us some privacy, please?"

The doctor and the two police officers looked at one another as if asking for each other's permission. The three of them turned around and left them alone in the room, closing the door behind them.

"Who was it, Sha? Who wanted you dead?" Cai was finding it hard to believe that Shahin knew who had done it and was still willing to fudge over the whole thing as if nothing happened.

Shahin pulled him in for another kiss, the lips to lips contact soothing Cai's nerves, calming him down.

"It was my mother."

Never in a million years had Cai expected to hear such a thing. He had considered maybe one of his siblings or a cousin. Not being welcomed in the Halcón household, Cai didn't know much about his relatives. He wouldn't be able to recognize most of them in a lineup. But as horrible as Shahin's mother was, he couldn't believe she would do something like that.

"I saw several bottles of Visine in the cabinet by the coffee machine. She buys a special brand of coffee just for me and her. We're the only ones in the family that like it. It's strong and bitter, and the rest of the family hates it." It was surreal to hear him talk about the whole sordid affair in such a calm, logical voice. "She must have spiked the coffee pods, knowing too well I'd be the only one drinking it."

Cai tried to talk a few times but he couldn't. It was as if a rock had lodged itself in his throat. He coughed a few times to clear it. "Why would she want her own son dead?" he managed to ask.

Shahin shook his head. "Not dead. Just sick." Cai frowned, confused. "Sick enough to believe that the curse was real."

Like a curtain Cai's confusion lifted. Of course, it made sense. "But this last time—you knew she was lying. Why would she do it again?"

"I never told her. She still thinks I don't know." Shahin leaned back on the pillows and brushed a hand over his face. "She was so determined to keep me away from you, she almost killed me."

"You're really not going to press charges against her?" Cai couldn't understand how a mother could do something like that. His own mom would have been horrified. It just didn't compute at all.

"She's my mother, Cai." Shahin brushed his hair with his fingers. "She's an awful woman, but she's my mother and the matriarch of my flock, the only surviving member from the old country. She's needed by all of us because she knows things about our kind no one else does. I can't do that to her or my people. I can't descend to her level."

Cai knew it wasn't going to be easy to convince the police officers, but he understood Shahin's reasoning. It still made his skin crawl to know the woman would be allowed to be the head of a whole family that depended on her for guidance and support. Shahin promised him there would be what he called *conditions* to his leniency, provisions put in place to make sure she didn't hold the bulk of the power and knowledge alone. All that power was making her lose track of common decency, apparently.

Later that day, and after an exhausting hour-long conversation with the police and the doctor, Shahin was released from the hospital. Still weakened by the effects of the poisonous substance, Shahin leaned on Cai's shoulder during the drive home. For a while, Cai thought he had fallen asleep, but as soon as he parked the car in front of his house, his mate stirred and looked up at him.

"Promise me one thing, Cai."

Cai would have promised him anything at that moment, as happy as he was that his soul mate was alive and well. "What?"

"Don't ever let me drink coffee at my mother's house again."

CHAPTER FOURTEEN

NEW BEGINNINGS

From up there, the world seemed insignificant, far away, meaningless. If it wasn't for the knowledge that Cai was down below somewhere, Shahin would be perfectly happy soaring through the skies, never changing into a human again. His mother's betrayal and his family's apathy had been the proverbial nail in the coffin for him. The only thing holding him to his human side was his soul mate.

Wings spread out fully, he glided through the air in slow motion, only moving his tail feathers once in a while to adjust his navigation. On the tip of each of his wings, the black feathers—darker than any others in his body—fanned until they were separated from each other, allowing him to manipulate his speed. He soared for hours, delighting in the feeling of the air beneath holding him up while the air above pushed him down. A game of opposing forces that resulted in his feathered body gliding in large circles high above the ground.

Today was the day he would face his mother. He had kept it a secret since his hospital stay a little over a week before. Cai had urged him to do it immediately, but he needed to have his full strength back, both physically and mentally. As much as he acted as if the fact his mother had nearly killed him wasn't that big a deal, he was hurting inside. The Halcón matriarch had never had a good relationship with her son. There were no memories of cuddles by the fireplace or a good night story, special cookies in the lunch box or a sympathetic shoulder to cry on. Mom was whom she was, and he had never dwelt too much on what could have been or what he had missed. But this was too much for even him to dismiss as just another quirk of her prickly personality.

Making a last loop around the lake, Shahin headed to his place and turned into his human form in one smooth move. He had long perfected what he called the morph-landing move: when he came for a landing and landed on feet, having changed seconds before he hit the ground. He rushed to the house, naked and cold, a nervous weight beginning to grow in the pit of his stomach.

For the first time in memory, Shahin rode his bike slowly and carefully. Not because he wanted to, but because he was too distracted by the thoughts plaguing his head. For once he was actually scared. Not of his mother, but of himself, of what he may say or do, what may transpire from such a conversation. Life-changing conversations like the one about to happen didn't always result in positive outcomes.

His mother was in the kitchen clipping coupons like she always did this time of the week. Their family had never lacked for funds, and yet the woman still felt the need to save money by carrying around hundreds of coupons every time she went shopping. Shahin shook his head as he approached from behind. She was alone. *Good. No one to witness the conversation.* In spite of it all, he still was reluctant to humiliate his mother in front of the flock.

"Mom, we need to talk." His mother turned around, startled. "Didn't mean to scare you."

She laughed, gathering the coupons on the table and dropping them into a small box by her feet. "You have to do a lot worse than sneaking up on me to scare me."

Anger sprouted in his gut. "What about if I told the cops you have been poisoning me with eye drops?"

Her whole body stiffened. "What are you talking about, boy?" Her voice went up an octave and her eyes bulged.

"You know exactly what I mean, Mother." Now that he had started, he was not about to stop. In some odd way, it felt good to let it out. "I've been sick as a dog thinking it was because of the damn curse while in truth you have been feeding me poison."

The Halcón matriarch giggled almost hysterically. "You have gone soft in the head since you started dating this full-human. What is this ridiculous story you're babbling about?"

"You told the whole flock a lie about mixed matings, fed it all these years, and when your own son found his soul mate in a full-human, you decided to do the unthinkable—poison me to make me believe in the curse." Anger was boiling now, growing wings. "What kind of a mother are you?"

The ashen hue of her face spoke volumes. He had hit a nerve. "What are you talking about? Lie? What lie? The curse is very much the truth. Ask any shifter."

"All the shifters in the eastern coast learned this story from you, Mom. You!" His voice rose to almost a yell. "Of course they believe it. Their leader told them this. But it was a lie, Mom. A terrible lie to prevent shifters from mating with full-humans."

"You can't prove it." Her lips trembled and she blinked rapidly as if trying to clear her vision. "You can't prove it."

"Oh but I can, Mother. I certainly can." He had planned to get to the point slowly, but now all he wanted to do was to go for the jugular. "You were married to a full-human, Mother. For almost seven years. Never got sick once." The tendons on her neck pulsed as if with a life of their own. "You had children with this man—me and my siblings. Why? Why this elaborate lie when you yourself mated with a full-human? That I cannot understand."

The woman he called mother threw her chin in the air and stood, her back straight and proud. "I did it to protect all my flock.

Full-humans are evil and dangerous."

"How can you say that, Mom? You were married to one." He was yelling now, his anger spilling out and taking flight. "He never hurt you, did he?"

"He did hurt me." She pressed a fist to her lips as to prevent any other words to come out. "He broke my heart."

It was as if someone had poured a bucket full of cold water over Shahin. He had never seen his mother look so vulnerable, so broken. Her shoulders drooped and she clutched her stomach with one arm. "Mom?"

"I was so in love with that man, I thought he was the one." She stuttered the words, eyes shiny with tears. "We were insanely happy for years. He had a little trouble dealing with the fact I was a shifter, but got used to the idea—or so I thought."

Shahin pulled a chair and sat next to her. Who was this woman who grieved for the loss of a loved one? What had happened to her thorny exterior, her rough shell?

"Then you were born—you and your siblings, all shifters. He couldn't handle it. He became more distant, disappeared for days at a time, refused to interact with you kids." Was she crying? "Then one day he left for good. Never called, never said anything. Just left a note telling me he couldn't live the rest of his life hiding from the other full-humans to protect his family."

Surprising himself, Shahin drew his mother into his arms in a comforting hug. "I'm sorry, Mom. I didn't know. He was obviously an idiot, a coward." She was crying in earnest now. "But not all humans are like that. Cai is not like that at all. And he is my soul mate, Mom. There is no mistaking the pull."

The Halcón matriarch looked up, eyes moist with tears, a hand against her chest. "I'm sorry, son. I don't know what I was thinking, making you so sick like that just to keep you away from Cai. I thought I was doing the right thing, that I was protecting you from unavoidable heartache." She brushed a hand over his cheek in an uncharacteristic caress. "Instead, I almost killed you. I'm so sorry. Will you ever forgive me?"

He nodded, unable to speak. His anger was gone, dissolved along with the first genuine tears he had seen his mother shed. Of course he would forgive her. She was the only mother he had, and in some way, he could understand why she did it. Not condone or even accept it, but understand it from the perspective of her wounded heart.

"You have to promise me one thing though." Shahin made himself focus on the practical and not let his unexpected sympathy for his mother cloud his mind. "You have to pick a group of younger shifters and share the truth about our people. True lore, Mom, not made-up stories or lies. Our flock can't be totally dependent on you to learn about our kind. It's not good for you either." *It gives you too much power and power is like wine—delicious and intoxicating.* But he didn't say it out loud. Instead, he squeezed her shoulder and smiled. "Agreed?"

She nodded and patted his hand. "Yes, I think you're right. It's time I let go of my anger and be the leader I'm supposed to be."

"Are you going to be sweet and accommodating from now on?" He chuckled, knowing all too well what the answer was going to be.

"Not a chance. I will let go of the grudge, but I can't turn vinegar into honey anymore than you can, son." She laughed, wiping a tear from her eye. "And if you tell anyone you saw me crying, I will pluck all your feathers. *Entiendes?*" Yes, he understood. Deep down inside he was glad. He didn't think he would have been able to handle a mom he didn't recognize anymore.

They talked for a while longer and then he got ready to go. He was anxious to go see Cai and tell him about what happened. He was already by the door when he turned around to look at his mother one last time. She was still sitting at the table, her hands loosely lying on her lap and her eyes lost in thought.

"And Mom, get used to Cai because he's not going anywhere." She looked up then, her eyes rounding in surprise, but still softer than they'd ever been. "He's mine and I'm his, and no force on this earth is going to separate us."

"YOU GOT TO BE KIDDING, Zack. I'm not going to have a brown cake at my wedding." Lyra threw her arms above her head, lips twisted into a frown, and her hair in a mess of tangles. Cai watched her from the corner of his eye, a smile on his lips. Zack was in so much trouble.

"But it's a Wookie cake—" The look he got from his fiancée would have melted a lesser being, but Zack had somehow channeled Yoda or some other Jedi and didn't seem as intimidated as he should have been. "You didn't want a Death Star so I thought Chewie since he's soft and cuddly."

"Soft and cuddly? The creature is a giant shaggy dog who wears weaponry as clothes." Cai's sister rose on her tiptoes, her face turning a virulent shade of red. "Listen to me, king of the geeks, there will be no Chewie or any other Star Wars creatures in my wedding. Everything will be white and silver, pure and beautiful."

"The stormtroopers have a white uniform." Zack was not about to give up on his idea. "And R2-D2 is white and silvery. He would make an excellent centerpiece for the tables."

Shahin watched the scene, his head slightly tilted to the side, and squinted. "This is fascinating. Are they always this entertaining?"

Cai laughed from his side of the couch. "You have no idea. They will be fighting like this until the moment they say 'I do.'" Lyra stomped out of the room, closely followed by Zack, still trying to convince her to include a Star Wars theme in the wedding. "You gotta love them."

Shahin turned to Cai and planted a kiss on his lips. "Not any more than I love you, Mr. Hot."

A subtle blush rose to Cai's cheeks. No matter how many times his boyfriend told him he found him attractive, he was still very uncomfortable and unsure of the idea. Compared to Shahin he was plain and even a bit dowdy with his white hair and lack of style. Wasn't that why he had always attracted older guys?

"You're putting yourself down in your head, aren't you?" Shahin had developed this eerie talent of being able to tell what he was thinking. Did soul mates share thoughts as well? He could have sworn that sometimes he did feel as if he knew exactly what Shahin was thinking. "Stop that, you hear? You are the hottest guy I've ever dated, and you don't even realize it."

Cai was just about to draw Shahin into another kiss when the bickering couple walked back in the room. The conversation had now evolved into where to spend the honeymoon, and options varied from a *Star Wars* themed hotel in California to a private beach property in Bali. It was obvious that the Christmas tree decorating had taken a back seat to their wacky wedding plans.

"Are they still wanting to get married on New Year's Eve?" Shahin asked, his voice a mere whisper.

"To say their vows right at midnight so they can have an anniversary in two different years." Cai chuckled. "Lyra has always been a bit—unusual, and I think she's marrying her match."

"Why don't we go upstairs to your room for a while and let

them duke it out?" Shahin lifted his eyebrows suggestively. "As funny as this whole conversation is, I can think of a few much more pleasurable things we could be doing to each other."

Cai pretended to be shocked. "With my baby sister down here?"

"Like she'll even notice us leaving. She's having way too much fun fighting with her fiancé." Shahin jumped to his feet and pulled on Cai's hand. "Come on. There is one thing I've been dying to try out." He winked, and Cai swelled with desire.

Shahin kept his promise. The "new" thing turned out to be extremely pleasurable for both of them. Cai was certain they'd try it again sometime soon. They rested in each other's arms afterward, breathless and happy, lying naked across the rumpled bed, their clothes strewn across the room.

"That was amazing." Shahin tried to catch his breath as he laid his head on Cai's chest. "Do you think your sister heard us scream?"

Cai sat up so quickly he almost sent Shahin flying off the bed. "Holy shit! My sister." He covered his face with a hand. "Oh, my God! We were loud, weren't we? Shit, shit—how am I going to look her in the eye again?"

Shahin got on his knees and moved behind his mate, massaging his well-shaped shoulders. "Come off it. She's an adult. Do you really believe she doesn't know what we were doing in here? Noise or no noise?"

"That's beside the point, Sha. She's my sister." Shahin was peppering his shoulders and neck with wet kisses, and his mind suddenly became very fuzzy again, his senses taking control. "Hell, Sha. You can drive me to distraction so easily."

Shahin laughed, and stretching around his mate, took Cai's lips with his. He suckled on Cai's lower lip before letting him go. "You're delicious and I can't get enough of you."

Cai turned and wrapped his arms around his mate's waist to bring him around and into his lap. As Shahin settled on his lap, Cai heard his name being called. "Lyra is calling me." Shahin looked at Cai with raised eyebrows. "Sorry. I have to go see what she wants. We can resume this later." He slid his lover off his lap and collected his clothes from the floor. He needed a very cold shower.

"What is it?" he yelled as he stuck his head out the room door. He didn't dare go downstairs yet. Not while his clothes couldn't hide what he preferred to keep from his sister.

"When you guys are done fucking up there, can you come down so I can show you something?" His sister never minced words. He blushed again, irritated that she could make him feel so embarrassed.

"We better go check it out or she'll never let go." They jumped in the shower for a quick cool down, got dressed, and came down to see what was going on.

To their surprise, the ceiling-high tree that they had bought together was completely decorated, and with silver lights flickering on, garlands decorating the walls and the mantel, and a funny-looking Christmas elf stood by the door. Lyra and Zack had been busy.

"This is what we can do when you two sex-crazed monkeys are not around to distract us." Lyra laughed and pulled Zack against her side. "We make an amazing team." Zack lifted a finger and opened his mouth to talk. "Don't even think about it, Zack. There will be no Darth Vader in the wedding reception and that's final."

"Holy crap, sis. This is awesome." Cai spun on his heels to look around him. "Thank you, Lyra."

Lyra smiled from ear to ear, hanging on to her fiancé. "Glad you like it. Now, according to our family tradition, you have to find a new ornament that symbolizes this last year and hang it on the tree."

"Can I pick one too?" Shahin seemed to be thoroughly enjoying the whole family holiday tradition. Cai doubted that his rather sour mother would have made his Christmases an occasion for sweet memories. On the other hand, Cai's mom had always loved Christmas and made each one a special time in her children's life.

"Of course," Lyra answered before Cai could. "You're part of the family now. You must pick your own ornament for the family tree."

Shahin smiled so brightly, the sun seemed to have landed in the room. Cai said a silent thank you for having him in his life.

"Let's go shopping." Cai laughed at his mate's enthusiasm. "I'm serious. I can't wait to get something for that tree."

"Tomorrow, Sha. It's almost eleven."

Lyra giggled and slipped into her coat.

"Thank you, sis. I love you."

Lyra stepped forward to kiss her brother. "I love you too, fool." Then, she pulled on Shahin's shirt and planted a kiss on his cheek. "And you are growing on me too, Mr. Hotness."

"Hey!" Zack laughed. "Watch it, woman. I'm standing right here."

Lyra turned to him and smiled. "Oh, you're cute too, my love." She looped her arm with his. "Let's leave the lovebirds alone."

Cai watched as his sister left through the door, her voice wafting over to him and Shahin. "No, you can't have Obi-Wan Kenobi either."

SHOPPING WAS NOT HIS THING. Other than the sporadic groceries, Shahin shopped very rarely. His closet was filled with very basic pieces of clothing, the result of his dislike for the activity. Since his work for the family business involved many hours online, he often did his shopping that way too. But this called for a special touch, a more personal one. He wanted to buy Cai an ornament that truly symbolized who he was, but he had no idea what he was going to get. He had looked through so many stores he couldn't remember which ones and was almost sure he was now visiting one for the second time.

Lyra had offered to come and help him, but he wanted to do this by himself. A true gift from the heart. *Shit. I wish I was better at this.* Every item in that shop blurred into the same thing. He needed to clear his mind and breathe some cool air.

"Shahin." He turned around to see his sister, Maya. "What a surprise to see you here. I don't remember you ever shopping."

He smiled and rubbed his day-old stubble. "I don't do it much. But I'm shopping for a special gift."

"For Cai?" He nodded. "I'm glad you guys found each other. Now that I know you're in no mortal danger from being with him, I'm very happy for you two."

Shahin was meeting Cai at the coffee shop in a few minutes. His mate had been very secretive about what he was doing in town and had refused to have Shahin keep him company. It was time he met some of Shahin's family.

"I'm meeting with him right now. Do you want to come and meet him?"

Maya's eyes lit up and she almost dropped the big package she had in her hands. "I'd love to. Are you sure?"

"Sure. I think it's time he meets my family." He relieved her from some of the weight she was carrying and they began walking down the street toward the train station. "How are things going at home?" He had not been to any of the family dinners since the day he ended up in the hospital. Even though he had forgiven his mother and wanted to believe she was fully remorseful and rehabilitated into decency, it still made him nervous to be anywhere around her for longer than a few minutes.

"Mom is Mom, but things have changed a bit." Maya balanced on her high heels, struggling with her shopping bags. "Can you believe that she has formed a committee of lore holders? She's been teaching them everything she knows about shifters, so that when she dies the knowledge will go on."

Shahin hid a smile behind his hand. "Well, that's progress. I'm proud of her for doing that."

Maya laughed. "There's more. She's finally sharing things about our father. He doesn't seem to have been the best of guys, but it is nice to know who gave us half our genes."

Entering the coffee shop, they were greeted by a burst of hot air. "Let's sit by the fireplace." It was Cai and his favorite seat.

"Did you know our father was a full-human?" Shahin was impressed that his mother was willing to share that too. They sat and arranged all her shopping bags by their feet. "Weird, don't you think? That she made up that story about cross-species matings? But at least she admitted it."

"Yes, I'm glad she did." He hadn't told anyone other than Cai about what he had learned from his mom. As long as she kept her promise, he would too.

"But what the hell was wrong with you then?"

"Some kind of bacteria I ingested apparently." He didn't like lying, but it wasn't too far from the truth.

They hadn't been there for long when Shahin saw Cai coming

in. His heart immediately did a little dance and his gut tightened. He could never quite get used to the effect his gorgeous boyfriend had on him. His mate spotted him and a smile stretched across his lips as he moved in their direction.

Shahin got up and kissed him. "Cai, this is my sister, Maya." She had also got to her feet and looked at him with a birdlike tilt of her head.

Cai shook her hand. "Hi. Nice to finally meet you, Maya."

After chatting for a while and ordering a few coffees, Shahin noticed Cai frequently putting his hand to the left side of his chest as if something was bothering him. "What's wrong?" He pointed at Cai's hand lying flat on his chest.

"This? It's nothing." Shahin looked at him, suspicious and curious at the same time. "Really. I'll show you later. What have you been doing with yourselves?"

"My sister has obviously been Christmas shopping," Shahin said with a chuckle, nodding toward all her shopping bags and packages. "I tried but failed miserably. Who knew shopping could be so complicated?"

"Cai, you should come and have dinner at our house." Shahin almost jumped off his seat. No way was he going to let Cai eat anything prepared in his mother's house. Cai laughed as if guessing what he was thinking. "Or maybe we could go to dinner together one of these nights?"

"I'd love that." Cai reached for his hand and gave it a squeeze.

"I'm so glad I got to meet you, Maya. I want you to know I love your brother more than anything else. I'll take good care of him."

Maya smiled. "No need to tell me. I can see it in the way you look at him. I couldn't be happier for you."

The day was winding down and the sun was already low on the horizon when they said their goodbyes and headed home together. Shahin had left his bike at Cai's place and driven to town with his mate. Even though a little miffed that he hadn't found the right gift for Cai, Shahin was looking forward to the evening with his soul mate, cuddling on the couch, making love, and talking the night away. It was the weekend and Cai didn't have to go to work the next day, which meant a languid, sensual, long night. No hurry, no pressure.

Cai unloaded the grocery bags in the kitchen and then joined Shahin in the living room. "I want you to go upstairs and wait for me. I have a surprise. A gift really."

Shahin threw his head back and laughed. "You little devil. Who would have thought?"

"Don't be cheeky." Cai caressed his face. "Just do as I ask you, please. I'll join you in a second."

There was no need for a second request. Shahin climbed the stairs, two steps at a time, anxious to get rid of all his clothing and anything else that may separate him from his mate.

When Cai entered the room, Shahin had stripped to his bare skin and was sitting on the edge of the bed. Cai drew a breath in and stepped closer to him, placing himself between his mate's legs.

"Undress me."

Shahin obeyed, beginning to strip him one layer at a time. On Cai's chest, there was a wide bandage that had not been there that morning. "What's this?"

"Take it off."

Slowly and carefully, Shahin pulled the bandage back to reveal what was underneath. He gasped as his mind made sense of what he was seeing. Cai had gotten a tattoo just below the shoulder and stretching over the left side of his chest. Still red and slightly swollen, it was the picture of a hawk in flight, its wings spread wide open as the bird soared over the magnificent landscape of his mate's body. Tears came to his eyes.

"It's your Christmas gift." Cai searched for his eyes and smiled. "A little early, but the tattoo parlor is not open on Christmas Eve. Your hawk over my heart as it should always be."

Laughing and crying at the same time, Shahin crossed his arms behind Cai's neck and held his forehead against his. "Thank you, Cai. I love it." Cai really loved him! His formerly blemish-free skin now exhibited a permanent sign of his love for Shahin. Better than rings or promises that could be broken; a tattoo was forever.

Pulling back, Shahin studied the tattoo again, rubbing his fingers gently over it. "It's a little tender." Cai chuckled. "Be gentle."

His hand explored further down from the tattoo to Cai's abs, curving around his waist, over his pants-covered narrow hips, and landed on tight glutes. "Is this gentle enough for you?" He cupped the muscles and squeezed gently through the thin fabric of his pants.

Cai took his mate's mouth with his in a long kiss. "You don't have to be *that* gentle," he whispered over his lips.

Shahin laughed and slid down Cai's body to unzip his pants and pulled them down, kissing the skin it revealed underneath. "You may regret having said that."

IT WAS STRANGE AND UNCOMFORTABLE talking to his dad. Ever since his mom's death, Cai's father had distanced himself from his own kids, both physically and emotionally. Lyra had been reluctant to let her brother call their dad and tell him about her impending marriage, but they had no other family around and it seemed wrong to have his baby sister get married without the surviving parent.

"I thought you might want to know, Dad." There was not much talking from the other end of the line. "I think it would mean a lot to Lyra if you could come."

"My baby girl is getting married." It wasn't a question. The now unfamiliar paternal voice came through the line as a whisper. "Does she really want me there?"

She would deny it, but Cai knew better. She still craved that close relationship she had had with their father before he left them. "Of course she does. You're her dad. You used to be so close."

There was silence for a moment, the only sound that of a soft whimpering of sorts. Was his father crying?

"I'm so sorry, Cai." For a moment Cai thought his father meant he was not coming. Not that he'd be surprised, but it was still hard to take. "I'm so sorry for having been absent from your lives all this time." *Wait! What?* "I've wanted to come back into your lives, but I wasn't sure I'd be welcome."

"Dad, you're our father. Why wouldn't we welcome you back?"

"Because I left you when you most needed me." His voice shook, and Cai's heart contracted. He had trained himself to not think of his father, not wonder why he had abandoned his own children and left him to hold down the fort, so to speak. He had never felt bitter or angry, but he had often wished things were different. "I was a mess, Cai. Just couldn't handle things without your mom. She was the love of my life, my everything. I loved—love you guys, but being around you reminded me of what I had lost. It took me a long time to get back on my feet."

The knot in his throat wouldn't let Cai speak. He had waited many years to hear his dad say that. Hard to believe this was really happening.

"I do want to come to my little girl's wedding," his dad continued. "I want to meet this man who won her heart. Is he a good guy?"

Cai nodded as if the man could see him. "Zack is a great guy.

Lyra couldn't have asked for a better man."

"I'm glad to hear that. Can't wait to meet him." His dad cleared his throat. "What about you, Cai? Do you have someone in your life?"

His father knew he was gay, but Cai also knew that it hadn't been as easy for him to accept it as it was for Mom. Cai had always got the impression that his dad thought he was going through a phase of some kind, and that one day he'd wake up and realize he was actually straight.

"I do. I met the love of my life, Dad. Just like you did when you met Mom."

There was silence first. "And who is it?"

Cai sighed. "My boyfriend is a great guy. He's the head of a marketing department and he's very successful." Why was he focusing on the part of Shahin's life he cared the least about? Shahin barely ever talked about his professional life because he didn't much care for it. His wild nature was more about the open spaces and the freedom of the skies than about how much money he made on a monthly basis.

"What's his name, son?" His father's voice had softened. "And does he love you back?"

Cai laughed, relieved. "Yes, he does love me. His name is Shahin."

They spoke for a while longer and then agreed on a date for his father's visit. It was a matter of some urgency since it was never easy to find plane tickets so close to the holidays. But it seemed the older Bane would move mountains if he had to, to be there for his daughter's wedding.

It was a weird coincidence that this long-wished-for conversation happened on the same day he was hosting a dinner for Shahin's closest relatives. Both his sister and brother were coming—without their families—and the family matriarch. Cai was very nervous about having Shahin's mom in his house. But not any more than his boyfriend was. The man was a nervous wreck. Cai knew that his mate wanted to believe his mother had her come-to-Jesus moment, but doubt still nagged him.

Cai had decided to cook instead of meeting them at some neutral restaurant in town. He'd gone shopping earlier and would start preparing the food soon. Lyra had promised to come and help him. Or sample the goods, like she always said. He had decided on a simple but satisfying meal of homemade lasagna and salad. His sister was going to pick up some cupcakes for dessert on her way over. Even though there were still a couple of hours before he needed to start the meal, he decided to go ahead and do it. It would keep his mind occupied and away from all the life-changing events that had been happening over the past three months.

The air was scented with the sweet smell of fennel and basil as the ground beef simmered on the stove. He had just begun chopping some onions for the salad when he heard a key turn in the lock and the door open.

"What's that smell?" He heard Shahin throw the keys on the cocktail table and stride to the kitchen.

"Dinner in progress." Shahin came from behind and hugged Cai, his lips nestling in the crook of his neck. "Don't distract the cook or we'll end up serving burnt pasta to your family."

Shahin kissed his neck loudly. "Nothing more than what they deserve," he said with a chuckle. "Why don't we just order pizza and go upstairs to make love instead?"

Cai laughed, his eyes burning from the onion juices. "Later, Sha. Later. Right now I want to wow your mother and siblings and make sure we don't all get poisoned by your mom." Shahin laughed. "Should we search her for bottles of Visine when she gets here?"

"We don't need it. Lyra is just as good with her laser eyes and bat hearing. She'll notice if anything goes awry." Shahin pulled away from Cai and picked an apple from the basket on the counter. "I have infinite faith in your sister's nosiness capabilities."

"I'll tell her you said that." Cai dropped the chopped onions in a bowl and covered it for later. From the fridge, he removed a container of ricotta, a couple eggs, and some fresh parsley. He set it all by the chopping board and searched for a bowl in the cabinet underneath. "Not sure she'll appreciate being called Her Nosiness, though."

Taking a huge bite of the apple, Shahin spoke through a mouthful. "She loves me. She won't care."

She did love Shahin. Cai was delighted that his sister had so totally accepted and welcomed the hawk-man into her heart. She had never been a fan of Jack or any of his other boyfriends. Like a mother hen, she was always suspicious of anyone trying to get close to him, and super protective. "You'll make a great father someday," he used to tell her as a joke, referring to the fathers in movies sizing up their daughters' dates.

"Are you going to help me or stand there munching away?"

"How can I help, my love?" Shahin patted his mate's bottom. "You know my talents are reserved for the bedroom."

Cai, relishing the heat Shahin's hand had left lingering on his backside, smiled. "You know what you've never told me?"

Shahin leaned against a cabinet across from the island where his mate was working. "What's that? I thought I had told you everything there was to know about my awesome person."

Snickering, Cai stirred the cheese and the eggs together. "Your age. You've never told me how old you are."

"Surely I did." He looked surprised. Cai shook his head and began chopping parsley with the precision of a chef. "I'm turning thirty tomorrow."

Cai dropped the knife, and in a misguided attempt at stopping it from falling to the ground, he grabbed for it and touched the sharp blade. Shahin dropped the apple and ran to his rescue, holding Cai's hand and studying the bleeding finger.

"Fuck, just what I need. Blood in the lasagna." Cai wiped his other hand on a towel, upset that he had allowed himself to be so startled by Shahin's news.

"I wouldn't worry so much. My family likes raw meat." He smiled wickedly and took Cai's finger to his mouth, licking the blood away. A fire roared inside Cai. Leave it to his boyfriend to make even a bloody finger feel sexy. "Yummy. Now, I've tasted you completely."

At that moment, he wanted nothing but to get naked with his lover, but there was a dinner to be cooked and very special guests to impress. "Tell me you're not a vampire as well."

Shahin wrapped the bleeding finger in a torn piece of paper towel. Switching his attention to another of Cai's fingers, he suckled it. Shivers shook Cai's whole body. *Damn you, Sha. I need to focus.* "No vampire here. Just a very skilled and sexy hawk."

Cai burst out laughing and pulled his finger away from him. "Make yourself useful, Mr. Cocky, and get me a Band-Aid. Your family might enjoy blood, but I know my sister doesn't." Shahin came back with one a few seconds later. "How come you didn't tell me your birthday was coming?"

"No one celebrates birthdays in my family. I just don't really think about it." Shahin picked up the discarded apple and began eating it again. "It's not important."

Cai bristled. "Of course it is. Birthdays are days to be celebrated by those who love you, Sha. You have a new family now and you need to share these things with me." He wrapped the Band-Aid around his thumb and threw away the wrapper. He chuckled under his breath. "I thought you were much younger."

Shahin's eyebrow shot upward. "How young?"

"Twenty-two, twenty-three…."

"Shifters carry their age better than full-humans," he explained. Then he looked at Cai from lowered eyelids. "You thought you were robbing the cradle, didn't you? I'm shocked, Mr. Bane. And slightly turned on by your wickedness."

While the meat cooked and with everything else mixed, chopped, and stirred, the couple sat in the living room, and Cai told Shahin about his phone conversation with his dad. Shahin listened with his usual attentiveness, as if Cai was the center of the universe and nothing else mattered. It made Cai feel special and loved like he'd never been before. Sure, he had dreamed about meeting someone who would put him on a pedestal and think of his needs before all else, but until Shahin, he had been the one doing all the giving and worshiping, and receiving none in return. It was so much better when all was reciprocated.

When Lyra arrived, hands filled with sweet-smelling boxes, and wrapped so tightly in a scarf it was a miracle she could breathe, the lasagna had been assembled and was baking in the oven. Cai had also prepared the salad and all he still needed to do was to set the table and dress the salad.

Lyra unwrapped herself and removed the artistic cupcakes from the boxes and placed them on a plate, nicely arranged so it looked like a rainbow.

"Those look delicious. Where did you get them?" Shahin asked, his nose sniffing the air around them.

"You better have a great Christmas gift for me, bro." She slapped Shahin's hand as he tried to stick a finger in the icing of one of the cakes. "I drove all the way to Confections to buy these." Cai pretended to be duly impressed and took his sister's coat and scarf to the guest room.

Zack was running a little behind, but he'd be there before dinner. "You know him—he can smell a good meal as far as the next county. He won't miss it."

Amid easy conversation and good company, Cai forgot who else was coming until the doorbell rang at precisely seven o'clock. His heart jumped up to his throat and he had to catch his breath. "They're here." He stole a glance at Shahin who smiled and winked. "It's going to be fine, right?"

Shahin lifted Cai's hand and kissed his knuckles. "It's going to be great. They'll be comatose from your delicious lasagna and won't have much to say."

Somehow Cai doubted that very much. The Halcón matriarch never seemed to lack anything to say.

THE AIR WAS SO THICK with tension, you could almost touch it. The Halcóns had arrived with their usual aplomb, Maya and Sal bickering loudly about which one would secure the babysitter for their children next and Mom yelling for them to shut up. When Cai opened the door, the talking stopped and silence ensued. It was so unexpected, they all stood as if paralyzed, not sure of what to do or say next.

"Are we playing the staring game?" It was Zack, arriving at that moment and peeking curiously from behind the three Halcóns.

Shahin couldn't hold it in any longer. He burst out laughing, followed by Zack who seemed to think this was the most hilarious scene ever. Cai, finally recovered from the shock, invited everyone to come in and led them to the living room.

"I hope my house was easy enough to find," Cai said, trying his hand at small talk, something Shahin knew he hated and dreaded.

"You have a lovely house." Maya looked around her, obviously curious to know how this man who had won her brother's devotion lived. "And beautifully located. You have woods in the back, right?"

The ice somewhat broken, they talked for a while until the oven bell rang reminding Cai that dinner was ready. Shahin stole glances at his mom who had so far remained silent and demure—two things his mother certainly wasn't. What was she up to? She wasn't fooling anyone. Even Cai, who didn't know her well.

Cai had made sure to set the table so that Mom sat between her two other children and away from Shahin. "There's no point in tempting the devil," he had said earlier.

"My brother makes the best lasagna this side of the Rockies." Lyra's protectiveness had made an appearance, much to Shahin's amusement. She shoveled a large slice of the exquisite-smelling dish onto her plate and passed it to Zack. "My mom taught him."

"And where is she?" It was the first time Shahin's mother spoke, her fork halfway to her mouth. "Does she live far?"

Shahin coughed, a piece of salad stuck in his throat. "Cai's mom passed away some years ago."

Mom seemed appropriately shocked. "I'm so sorry to hear that. I'm sure you miss her."

Not quite knowing what to make of this new attitude from his mom, Shahin just kept stuffing his mouth with forkfuls of lasagna and darting glances from one person to another as if expecting something to suddenly explode.

"Shahin tells us that you spend part of your year in Canada." Lyra didn't seem fazed about any of the tension and prattled on as usual. "That has to be very inconvenient, moving your whole family like that twice a year."

"We're used to it and we carry very little with us." Maya was the only one of the three that was at ease making conversation. "We leave pretty much everything behind."

"That's just wild!" Lyra's eyes widened and she turned to Zack. "Can you imagine, traveling that light? That's awesome, Maya. But do you have to move or can you just decide to stay for a change?" Lyra sneaked a peek at her brother.

"There's no hard-set rule," Shahin answered, his eyes roving to Cai and a smile playing on his lips. "You can go, you can stay… it's your choice. Especially for me, since my job is done in cyberspace." Shahin noticed with satisfaction the smile his statement elicited from his boyfriend.

Even though everyone was on their best behavior, Shahin was happy when the night came to an end and his family prepared to leave. At the door, and before she left, Shahin's mother turned to Cai. "I want to apologize to you, Cai, for trying to keep you away from my son." The two men stiffened, afraid of what she might say. "Now that I've seen you together, I understand—you are indeed soul mates. Don't let anyone tell you otherwise. I'm ashamed of what I've done and this is the only time you'll hear me say that. But I do regret the terrible things I did and said." She smiled the rarest of smiles and left, following her other two children who were already down the stairs and on the walkway.

Both Shahin and Cai were stunned, holding on to each other in the doorway. "Well, that was—unexpected," Cai said.

"Hell, it was historic." Shahin laughed, closing the door. "She's not kidding when she said this would be the only time she said that. She managed to totally behave tonight. I'm reluctantly impressed."

"We're leaving too, bro." Lyra had icing from a cupcake on her nose. Cai wiped it with his finger. "I'm stuffed and need to walk a little to digest. Zack and I are going to walk by the station. Wanna come?"

Cai looked at Shahin, a small smile lifting the corner of his mouth. "Nuh, not this time, sis." He reached out for his mate's hand. "We have a birthday to celebrate, Sha and I."

Shahin started. "What?"

Cai lowered his voice so only his boyfriend could hear. "Tonight is your night, Sha. I'm going to make sure you'll never forget it." The promise in Cai's voice made him shiver in anticipation. He couldn't have wished for a better birthday present.

CHAPTER FIFTEEN

CHRISTMAS SURPRISES

"I'll be late today." Cai slipped his coat on and picked up his gloves and scarf from the chair. "We'll just order in when I come back."

Shahin, still lying in bed with tablet in hand, looked up. "Pizza?" Desire stirred in Cai's body as he scanned his boyfriend's sexy body, half stretched on the bed, chest bare, propped against two pillows. "Shall I order around seven?"

Cai swallowed hard, finding it hard to speak all of a sudden. This was not the time. He had to be at work in less than thirty minutes, and now all he wanted to do was get undressed and show his lover exactly how much he loved him.

Shahin put the tablet beside him on the bed and glanced at him, a mischievous smile on his lips. "Unless you play hooky today."

Damn you, Sha.

"I'm leaving before you lead me down the wrong path." Scarf tightly wound around his neck, Cai moved away from the bed. "Love you, but I got to get to work. With Christmas break coming soon I have to finish this project ASAP."

Putting on a pretend and comical pout, Shahin whined. "I better not kiss you goodbye then."

"Leaving—" With a wave, Cai rushed out of the room and toward the front door. If he stayed even a few more minutes, he was sure to end up in bed with his incorrigible boyfriend. He yelled out, "Goodbye, hawk-man."

Lately, he felt more and more reluctant to go to work and leave Shahin behind. He wondered if this happened with every couple in love and if it ever faded away. As inconvenient as it was to be aroused most of the time and spend hours wishing for the end of the workday, he loved it—the feeling of belonging somewhere with someone, of the warm and exciting feelings Shahin stirred in him with a simple look. It was a mix of agony and ecstasy, and he now wondered how he had been able to live his whole thirty-five years without it.

At work, he made himself focus on the project, often consulting with Ted and Eliza, revising and redrawing until it had reached what he thought was an unacceptable quality. A quick glance at his watch told him it was almost time to clock out. Unlike most days, when he would drive home as fast as he could within the law and throw himself into Shahin's arms, today he had other plans. Ted was going to help him pick a ring for Shahin. It made him all kinds of nervous to think about what he was contemplating doing at Christmas. Anxiety rose in his throat at the mere thought of asking for his boyfriend's hand in marriage. Shahin was such a wild creature who obviously adored the freedom of flying and the thrill of speed; how would he react to such a tethering proposal?

"Are you ready, Cai?" Ted had his coat on already. In spite of his earlier misgivings about Cai's relationship with Shahin, he had been very supportive and encouraging. "I've seen how happy you are with him. The happiest I've seen you in a long time," he had said.

"Sure." Cai turned off his laptop, closed it, and followed his friend into the cold. "Where are we going?"

"My friend, Caitlin, runs a jewelry shop just down the street. She'll hook you up."

As promised, the store was just a couple blocks away, and Ted's friend was very willing to help with the selection. After almost an hour of heart-wrenching indecision, he settled on a gold band with an onyx overlay. It was simple and modern. Shahin would like it.

"I'd kill for a cup of hot coffee right now," Ted said, pressing the lapels of his coat against his chest.

Cai wanted to run home, but his friend had gone out of his way to help him. A cup of coffee was the least he could do to repay him.

"Let's go to Jirani's then."

The fire roared in the hearth and a small crowd of people in their winter gear lent their warmth to the large coffeehouse. They ordered two cups of coffee and sat at a table to drink it.

"So, you're going to do it?" Ted cradled his hot cup between his hands.

Cai took a long sniff of the delicious brew before taking it to his lips and sipping it. "Yes, I have no idea if it's the right thing, but it's what my heart is telling me to do."

"You guys have really hit it off then?" Ted leaned in and covered Cai's hand with his. "You look so happy."

At the thought of every feeling Shahin always stirred up in him, Cai smiled. "I am happy. Sha is my soul mate, and I want to spend the rest of my life with him. I hope he shares my feelings."

Ted patted his hand. "If he doesn't, he's a fool."

"So, this is what you do after work." Shahin's voice, unexpected and surprising, startled Cai.

Shahin stared at Cai's hand still under Ted's. The look in his eyes could have liquefied rocks. Cai pulled his hand away. "Sha. What are you doing here?"

"Apparently catching you in the act." The hawk-man's voice was a low growl. Cai had never heard him talk in that tone of voice. It scared him.

"What do you mean?" What did he think Cai was doing there?

True, he hadn't told him he was meeting Ted after work. How could he? Telling him the truth would mean ruining the surprise.

The expression of pure hurt in Shahin's face pierced his heart like a hot skewer. He wanted nothing more than to jump to his feet and wrap his arms around his boyfriend to assure him everything was all right.

"I came here for coffee and hoping to surprise you at work. You know, the place you're supposed to be working late?" Shahin spat out the words as if they burned his tongue. "How could you be cheating on me with your old boyfriend?"

Cai stood up so fast, his chair slid across the floor behind him. The other patrons turned their attention to them. He didn't care. "It's not like that at all, Sha. You're so wrong if you think I'd be unfaithful to you."

"Fuck you, Cai." Shahin turned around and ran out of the coffee shop, his progress followed by every eye in the store.

Stunned, he stood in the middle of the coffee shop, the center of everybody's attention. Cai shook as sadness and a painful sense of dread assailed him. *What do I do? What just happened?*

"Cai, what are you waiting for? Go after him, for God's sake." Ted snapped him out of his near paralysis, a hand on his arm. "Go. Don't let him go."

Returning to reality, Cai gave his friend a grateful smile and left running. Emerging from the store, he spied Shahin sprinting through the parking lot across the rails. Cai took off running. He needed to get to him before his boyfriend jumped on his bike and left his life forever.

"Sha, wait," he yelled across the way. "Please, let me explain."

Shahin stopped and turned around. The shadows under the streetlights obscured his handsome face, not allowing Cai to see it clearly. Was he still hurt? Did he hate him?

Whatever he was feeling, Shahin waited for him, his lean, strong body stiff and coiled. "What do you want? What is there to explain? That after all these years you realized you missed your high school boyfriend? I guess it's true what they say about your first—you never forget them."

Cai had reached Shahin and longed to touch him. "I'm not cheating on you, Sha. I'd never do that."

"I guess going out with an old boyfriend while your current one waits for you at home does not count as cheating." Cai could see his face now, still half hidden by the darkness. He loved that face—deep-set eyes protected by thick eyebrows, a perfect aquiline nose, and well-defined lips that begged to be kissed often and hard. He hated that he was the reason pain was now contorting those beautiful features.

"I did lie to you—for a good reason." Cai caught himself as he reached out to touch his boyfriend. "Ted was helping me prepare a Christmas surprise for you."

Shahin snorted, his arms crossed protectively over his chest. "Mission accomplished. I was surprised."

Not able to control himself any longer, Cai gripped Shahin's arm. "Sha, I love you. I'd never—"

With a sudden yank, Shahin pulled away from Cai's grasp. "Save yourself the trouble. I've been lied to enough to last me a lifetime."

Not seeing any other way out of it, Cai dug into his pocket for the small ring box and went down on his knee. The paved parking lot was freezing cold, but he didn't feel a thing. Shahin was staring at him as if he had gone bonkers.

"I wanted to save this for Christmas, but you leave me no other choice." Cai opened the box and handed it to Shahin, whose eyes seemed about to pop out of their sockets. "Sha, my love, will you marry me?"

Silence descended on the world. All the background noise of a minute ago—people talking, cars driving by, music drifting from afar—dissolved into nothing. They were the center of the universe, their hearts beating in unison. Shahin gasped and then fell silent, staring wild-eyed at the ring in his hand.

"Will you, Sha? Will you please be mine forever? For better, for worse, for richer, for poorer, in sickness and health, until death do us part?"

Shahin began to thaw. He licked his lips, uncrossed his arms, and then fell on his knees in front of Cai. "When did you—?"

"Ted was helping me pick a ring for you," Cai explained, relief beginning to wash over him. "He's just a friend, Sha. You are my love."

Shahin threw his arms around Cai's neck and drew him in for a hug. "I'm sorry I didn't trust you. I should have known better."

Pulling back, Cai brushed his free hand over his mate's face in a gentle caress. "You have nothing to apologize for. It was an honest mistake."

Their lips joined, tongues moving together in their usual sensual dance. "I love you, Cai."

"Well, will you?"

"Marry you?" Shahin grabbed the ring from inside the box and handed it to Cai. "Not until you put a ring on it."

Laughing, Cai slipped the ring onto Shahin's finger, caressing his hand as he did it. "And now?"

Shahin looked at the ring in his finger and smiled. "Shit, Cai. Of course I'll marry you."

Still kneeling by Shahin's motorcycle, and involved in a passionate kiss, the couple didn't notice the first snowflakes of the season drifting slowly and silently from the sky, falling on top of the two, light-as-a-feather blessings from the heavens above.

HE'D ALWAYS WONDERED WHAT ABOUT flying attracted him besides the obvious exhilaration of height and the feeling of floating above everything else. That Christmas morning, he finally understood. Inside the rebel, the one who always went the extra mile to be contrary and against the norms, there was someone who loved peace and quiet.

With his fiancé curled up against him in bed, Shahin watched as the snow fell outside the window in great silent flakes. It had started snowing when they went to bed the night before, so they left the curtains in the bay window opened to watch it coming down. Now, he could lie back and enjoy the view. Cai's room faced the back of the house, where the privacy of the woods protected it from unwanted attention. Where before there was only green now there was white—pure, untouched snow covering the landscape with its soft, cold mantle. In the house all was quiet, Cai's gentle breathing the only sound breaking the soothing silence snow always brought along.

A sigh escaped his lips as he wished he could stay like that forever, skin to skin with his man, happy in the knowledge he was loved, safe within his arms. He had never been one to need protection of any kind; neither did he ever feel in danger other than from his natural predators. But he recognized now that his "wild oats" had been nothing but a way to mask the insecurities and fears of never being truly loved. His upbringing hadn't been what anyone could call loving. In his mind the memory of his mother throwing him off the ledge of the mountain as soon as she deemed him ready to morph and fly still haunted his dreams. He had fallen dozens of feet, picking up speed with nothing to hold him but terror, until his instincts kicked in. His body changed to that of his hawk for the first time and swooped up a few short feet from hitting the ground. "It's the way of the hawk," his mother had said. Maybe that was true, but he wasn't a full-hawk. His human side was but a small child in need of support and care.

"What are you sighing about?" Cai stirred against him, his eyes still unfocused from sleep. "Did something happen?"

Shahin leaned over and kissed him. "Nothing is happening. That's what's so great." He brushed his palm against the stubble on Cai's face. "I love being here with my boyfr—I mean, fiancé."

Cai shuffled upwards until his head was nestled in the crook of Shahin's neck. "You always smell good in the morning. How do you manage that?"

"Fresh air and good living." Shahin laughed at his own joke. "Maybe it's a hawk thing, even though birds are not known for their great smell." He snorted.

"Whatever it is, I'm thankful for it. My old boyfriend smelled like rotten fruit in the morning." Cai chuckled and gave his skin another sniff, as if smelling perfume. "Please, tell me I don't smell like a drunken raccoon."

"I've never smelled one, but you smell amazing." Shahin's smile faded and his eyes blurred a bit. "You smell of promises and hope. Like home."

Lost in a kiss and then another, they didn't notice the passage of time. When Shahin glanced at the clock and realized it was already early afternoon, he hopped out of bed. "There is something I want to do with you today. Before it gets dark."

Lyra was coming for dinner, after spending Christmas Day with Zack's family in DC. Cai had promised her a light meal of sandwiches and butternut squash soup instead of the lavish meal he had been planning for all of them. "Zack's mom always cooks enough for a small army," she had said on Christmas Eve. "I'll be more stuffed than a sausage by the time I come to your place." The afternoon was theirs for the plucking, no rush, no stress. Cai had cooked the soup the night before and the sandwiches would be prepared on the spot.

Shahin threw a glance at Cai, still in bed, and frowned. "What are you waiting for? Let's get dressed."

After a quick shower together, they got dressed in a hurry. Shahin instructed Cai to bring an empty overnight bag, and Cai raised an eyebrow. "Whatever for?"

"To carry my body after you kill me with your kisses." Shahin never even blinked.

"Man, you used to be cool," Cai joked, stuffing his arms into the sleeves of a black peacoat. "Now you're just cheesy."

Shahin laughed, and with a scarf tied around his neck he opened the door and pulled his fiancé along with him into the cold, snowy afternoon.

"You're driving," he told Cai as they hopped down the stairs to the snow-covered sidewalk.

Throwing the empty bag on the back seat, Shahin settled beside Cai for the drive. "Where exactly are we going?" Cai maneuvered his car out of the parking space and onto the road.

Shahin twisted an imaginary mustache, raised an eyebrow like Groucho Marx, and said in a thick voice, "Just follow my lead."

His mood had never been this bubbly, not even when he had partaken in too much wine—which he often did before meeting his soul mate. But now, this almost childish joy percolated in his chest, filling him with the sense that nothing could go wrong. Ever.

Following Shahin's directions, Cai drove the car to the Shenandoah mountains, an hour away and parked. "Are you going to throw us both off the mountain again in that silly wingsuit of yours?" Cai didn't seem too excited about the possibility.

"No, I just want you to see something." Shahin left the car, a swing in his step, and came around to pull Cai out. "Come on."

Shahin took them to the edge of the mountain just like he had done that fateful day. Cai looked down the mountainside. It was beautiful but a vertiginous fall into the woods below.

"This is my Christmas present for you," Shahin said, weaving his fingers through Cai's. "I wanted to give you something special like you gave me, but I couldn't find anything that felt right."

"You don't need to give me anything, Sha." Cai pulled him

closer, the mist of their breaths mingling together between them. "You've given me so much already."

"But I haven't given you all of me. Not yet." Cai squinted his eyes, the skin crinkling in the corners. Shahin smiled. "You know the human side of me, but you're yet to meet my hawk."

Cai waved a hand in the air as if dismissing the idea. "You're one and the same. I love the man and the hawk."

"I know. But I want to share this part of me with you too. I want you to know me whole, inside and out, my good side and my bad." He leaned over and planted a brief kiss on Cai's lips. "My human and my hawk."

"How are you going to do that?"

Instead of answering, Shahin dropped Cai's hand and began undressing quickly, shedding all his clothes in the fresh snow. "Make sure you take my clothes back."

"As much as I love your enthusiasm, Sha, this is neither the place or the time for sex." Cai smiled, watching his lover's lovely body appear one inch at a time from underneath the clothes.

"No sex right now," Shahin said with a wink, dropping the last piece of clothing on top of the pile. He stood naked and shivering in the freezing cold. "After you watch it for a while, drive back home and wait for me in your backyard. I'll come to you there."

"Are you sure about this? It's so cold."

Pulling his boyfriend in for another kiss, Shahin laughed. "Sure.

I love you, Cai. This is for you." Turning toward the edge, Shahin opened his arms and threw himself off the precipice. He heard Cai's sharp intake of breath and then he felt the familiar pull and tug of his body changing—feathers sprouting, body shrinking and adjusting in shape and weight, wings replacing arms. As soon as the metamorphosis was complete, he soared up to where he could see his lover staring at him with wonder in his eyes. He swooped down and around Cai a few times, delighting in his mate's reaction, and then flew away to allow Cai to get in the warm car and drive home. His human heart blended with his hawk's and sang for joy. He now could finally say he had shared himself fully with the love of his life.

IT WAS STRANGE AND WONDROUS all at the same time. To witness Shahin's transformation from a tall man to a majestic hawk would never be easy to describe. As his body changed, shifted and distorted like a piece of clay in the hands of a sculptor, Shahin's handsome male figure was replaced by an equally exquisite graceful animal, his body covered in gray and reddish feathers. Cai had the sudden urge to paint it, to immortalize it on canvas. The only thing distinguishing Shahin's hawk from others was his eyes—not the usual brown of the birds of prey, but the azure of the ocean on a sunny day.

Shahin took one last loop around Cai, the cold draft from his large wings making Cai shiver. He was magnificent. Words couldn't describe what he was feeling at the moment: grateful, happy, proud, but most of all honored to have been chosen to share Shahin's metamorphosis.

As soon as he saw Shahin flying away from the mountain, he knew it was time to drive home. He got in his car and drove faster than usual all the way to his house, grateful for the sparse traffic of Christmas Day. He parked by the house and ran inside, grabbed a blanket, and went directly through the back door into his backyard. The evergreen trees in the back and between him and his next-door neighbors provided his townhome with the privacy he enjoyed and needed so much. He would wait outside for his boyfriend to come home, no matter how cold it was.

The snow had stopped some time ago, but the air was frigid as the evening rolled in, the blue sky turning darker. Cai began to worry. Shahin had been attacked by an owl before when flying at night. He hoped that he would come home before night arrived. Shahin had told him his hawk was aware of his human side, but did his human really have full control over what the hawk decided to do? He still had so many questions, but right then all he wanted was to have him back with him.

In the distance, Cai heard the unmistakable call of the hawk, and a pair of great wings appeared on the horizon, closing in with great and graceful flaps. The hawk swooped down, closer and closer until it almost touched the ground in front of Cai. Suddenly the talons became human feet and the wings turned to arms. Shahin was standing barefoot in the snow mere inches from him. Cai, his heart beating a frenzied rhythm inside his chest, swung the blanket over his very human mate's naked body and pulled it until glued to his, wrapping the blanket around Shahin.

"That was amazing." Cai's lips lingered over his fiancé's, his hands caught between them. "Thank you."

"You're not spooked by the weirdness of it all?" Shahin shivered against Cai, warm breath tickling his nose.

Cai smiled, dropping a kiss on his nose. "It was like a miracle. What's there to be spooked about? It was like watching a butterfly turning into a different butterfly—equally beautiful and miraculous."

"I'm all yours now, body and soul," Shahin said, and then added with a chuckle, "Both bodies."

Cai didn't give him time to say anything else. Covering Shahin's mouth with his, Cai traced the edges of his mate's lips with his tongue. His cold lips still tasted of fresh air and evergreens, pure heaven.

Breathless, Cai pulled away. "I only have one body to give you, but it's all yours."

With a wink and a lick of the lips, Shahin squeezed himself closer to Cai. "And what a body that is. Who needs two?"

Their lips joined again and for a while, they stood blissfully unaware of the freezing temperature, warmed by their body contact and the happiness coursing through their veins. When they finally pulled apart, Cai stared into his lover's deep blue eyes and smiled.

"I love you, Shahin Halcón," he whispered. An overwhelming wave of love ran through him. "Did you know, Sha, that in your eyes I can see the blue of the skies above and the oceans below?"

"And in yours, I see the promise of happiness. You're my own happy ever after, Cai."

Cai turned around and they walked side by side into the house, two men, one soul—the hawk and his lover walking together toward the infinite blue of their future together.

THE END

THANK YOU

Thanks for reading *Infinite Blue*. I do hope you enjoyed Shahin's and Cai's story. I appreciate your help in spreading the word, including telling a friend. Before you go, it would mean so much to me if you would take a few minutes to write a review and share how you feel about my story so others may find my work. Reviews really do help readers find books. Please leave a review on your favorite book site.

Don't miss out on New Releases, Exclusive Giveaways and much more!

Newsletter: www.eepurl.com/b97Q3P

Facebook: www.facebook.com/authornatalinareis

Facebook reader group: www.facebook.com/
groups/215263965917134

Twitter: @TichaB

Pinterest: www.pinterest.com/lisboeta62

Goodreads: www.goodreads.com/author/show/14883335.
Natalina_Reis

Instagram: https://www.instagram.com/reisnatalina

Website: www.catarinadeobidos.wordpress.com

Email: catarinadeobidos1@gmail.com

ABOUT THE PUBLISHER

Hot Tree Publishing opened its doors in 2015 with an aspiration to bring quality fiction to the world of readers. With the initial focus on romance and a wide spread of romance subgenres, we envision opening up to alternative genres in the near future.

Firmly seated in the industry as a leading editing provider to independent authors and small publishing houses, Hot Tree Publishing is the sister company to Hot Tree Editing, founded in 2012. Having established in-house editing and promotions, plus having a well-respected market presence, Hot Tree Publishing endeavors to be a leader in bringing quality stories to the world of readers.

Interested in discovering more amazing reads brought to you by Hot Tree Publishing? Head over to the website for information:

WWW.HOTTREEPUBLISHING.COM